# MURDER AT THE PAISLEY PARROT

A MARSHALL JAMES NOVEL

MARK McNEASE

Published by MadeMark Publishing
Stockton, New Jersey
www.MadeMarkPublishing.com

ISBN 10: 1979581894
ISBN 13: 9781979581899

Cover design by MadeMark Media
Cover image licensed from Depositphotos

Praise for *Last Room at the Cliff's Edge*

"Nathaniel Hawthorne wrote that "easy reading is damn hard writing." McNease writes in this ostensibly effortless way, employing all the elements of a true story teller: intrigue, tension, memorable characters and perfect pacing. I also admire the ease with which he captures a woman's point of view. Linda is heroic and flawed and utterly believable."

Jean Ryan, author of *Survival Skills* and *Lost Sister*

"This suspenseful series launch from McNease (the Kyle Callahan Mysteries) introduces retired homicide detective Linda Sikorsky ... Plausible sleuthing and smart characterizations combine for a winner."

Publishers Weekly

**Also By Mark McNease**

**Audiobooks**
Murder at Pride Lodge
Pride and Perilous
Death by Pride
Death in the Headlights
Last Room at the Cliff's Edge
Stop the Car

**Mysteries and Thrillers**
Murder at Pride Lodge
Pride and Perilous
Death in the Headlights
Death by Pride
Kill Switch
Last Room at the Cliff's Edge

**Other Books and Writing**
Stop the Car: A Kindle Single
The Seer: A Short Story
Rough & Tumble: A Dystopian Love Tragedy
An Unobstructed View: Short Fiction
5 of a Kind: More Short Fiction

## ACKNOWLEDGMENTS

This time it's a little different. The people I want to thank are all dead: Little John, Robert, David, Gina Rae, Lon, and Jim, whose presence next to me for four years went devastatingly cold in November, 1991. There are many, many more names I could add, but it would be as exhaustive as it is exhausting. My youth—or, more accurately, my young adulthood—was spent in a perpetual state of mourning. So many men I knew were here one week and gone the next. That was our reality.

It's a history worth preserving, but not something to be upset about when succeeding generations forget. We all forget. Vietnam? What was that? Richard Nixon? Who was he? A plague called AIDS? What relevance does that have to us?

It's okay. Time does indeed march on, and all of us, and all we will know, fall beneath its boots.

'Murder at the Paisley Parrot' and what will be the Marshall James series, is not really about AIDS or bringing to life a past that is best left buried, though not forgotten. Rather, the stories take place in a particular time, when death was as common as news of an oncoming storm. When death itself was an oncoming storm, but one that lasted for years and left only fragile lives to be rebuilt in its wake.

So I acknowledge the men, women and children who lived through it, and the tens of thousands who did not. In a story set in a bar, let's raise a toast to them.

*In memory of the Lemon Twist bar.*
*Make mine a double.*

# PROGNOSIS

THERE'S A SOUND TO NEW YORK CITY that never goes away. It's not exactly white noise—that seems too clean for a place this filthy—but a perpetual hum that matches the eternal grayness of the night sky. When you spend significant time here, if you're the least bit conscious of your surroundings, you realize after a while that you can't see the stars and there is no such thing as true silence. New York City, especially Manhattan, is a relentless sensual assault. You see it even when you don't; you hear it at all times, and, in the summer, as it is now, you *smell it*. That is its most inescapable trait from June through August. You can forget about stars you haven't seen since you were last off the island, and you can marvel at what passes for quiet at 3:00 a.m., but you can't ignore the smell of the place. Ripe. Rotten. The way you imagine a body smells when maggots are halfway through their meal. The greatest city in the world.

All of it—the sounds, the sights, the smells—waft through my second-floor window like hot air in a slow updraft. This is especially true every Tuesday, also known as trash day, when the building superintendent and his helper of the week (they change almost as often as the girlfriends of the drag king next door) haul out a dozen trash bags and pile them by the curb. Clear plastic ones for the recyclables, the rest a dark brown, the kind they find torsos and arms stuffed into every now and then along the highway. No corpses in ours yet, just a week's worth of Chinese takeout, cat litter, shitty diapers, and everything else we discard from our lives on a daily basis. There it sits, for a day and a night, basting in its own putrid juices until the garbage truck comes along in the morning waking everyone up, jamming traffic for a half hour as it crawls trash pile to trash pile.

Ours seems to give off especially toxic fumes. Knowing that all odors are particulate, I keep my windows closed from Monday mid-day to Tuesday late morning. But it still seeps in, it still invades my home. Between the smell of summer waste and the exhaust from buses snaking up 40th Street to the Port Authority bus terminal across the avenue, it's amazing my lung cancer came from smoking and not from living on this corner.

I'm a cancer survivor, not a combatant. I hate the way illness gets anthropomorphized, turned into some cognizant *thing*, a boxer in the ring with us. We've got the charity-approved pink boxing gloves on, and that cancer, that tumor, weighing in at a slim one-sixty and wearing the black trunks with the skull and crossbones, faces off against us in the title match of our lives. I never saw my cancer as an opponent or in any way conscious of what it was doing to me. I did not fight, at least not in any metaphorical sense. I just did what I was told to do, lived through the chemo and the surgery that took out a quarter of my left lung, and, to everyone's great surprise, outlived my six-month prognosis by two and a half years.

Yes, it's been three years since I first coughed up blood. It's been almost that long since I enjoyed a Marlboro and a glass of bourbon—where I come from there's no such thing as whiskey without a cigarette. And it's been that long since I told my oncologist to take her dire prediction and shove it, in a nice way. We're friends, so far as a man and his cancer doctor can be, but Dr. Lydia Carmello fully expected me to die when she said I would. She usually gets it right, and she's not the sort of person to credit miracles. She's a hard case, that one. She's had to be. Death is the nightcap in her profession, after an evening of chemo and a meal of surgery for the ones who can be operated on. She assumed I would be one of her regulars—treated, comforted, referred to some support group where I could mourn the loss of myself while I was still around to do it—but nothing special. Then six months came and went. Nine months. A year. Two years.

And finally, when I'd been in remission through the birth of Dr. Carmello's daughter and the celebration of her first birthday, to which I was not invited, Lydia declared me an anomaly and said I just might get old after all. At fifty-eight I'm not that far from it, but she meant truly old, Social Security and Medicare old, the kind of old when saying you're as young as you feel just makes you look foolish. Neither of us is counting on it, given the return rate of stage three lung cancer, but it's nice to have possibility in your life.

I've had plenty of that, by the way: possibility. I was a kid who could have been something, given a chance. Too bad I never was. At least not early on, growing up in Indiana in a place too big to be a town and too small to be a city.

Elkhart in the 1960s and 70s was a bustling community of 30,000 or so Hoosiers. They headed to work at the Conn band instrument facility, or one of the motor home factories that gave Elkhart its claim to fame. We once had the highest concentration of millionaires in the country. It may not have lasted long, but it was something to be proud of. We were the RV Capital of the World. It still is as far as I know—who wants to compete for a title like that?—but I can't confirm it, since I haven't lived there in forty years. I went back to sell my father's house twenty years ago and that was the last I saw of Elkhart.

Indiana was a place to flee when I was young. For a gay kid who came out at the age of sixteen, Elkhart was not welcoming. It didn't matter that I was a native son, or that my family had been there for several generations. A queer is a queer is a queer, to paraphrase Gertrude Stein, and I was certainly one of those. I announced my sexuality in high school, survived the hostile and sometimes violent reaction of my peers, and got the hell out two days after graduation. My mother was already dead. My father was drunk and on his way to an early grave. My sister and brother were old enough to fend for themselves, and I was ready to get as far away as I could.

I'd seen a report on *60 Minutes* about homosexuals in

Hollywood. Or maybe it was specifically about homosexual prostitutes. I don't remember exactly, but I recall being transfixed—not by the segment itself, which was judgmental of the seedy, sad lives of L.A. hustlers—but by the fact they existed. What was a hustler? I wondered. Where did they come from? What exactly did they do for money? I had an idea, having some experience myself by then, although it all involved high school classmates and no money was exchanged. But this was exotic. Alluring. And exactly where I went when I packed my belongings into my orange Gremlin, put the clutch in drive and pulled out of my dad's driveway for the last time, returning only for short visits over the years until I went back to plant a 'For Sale' sign on the lawn. I wouldn't have gone then, except my sister and brother refused to deal with it and somebody had to bury the old man.

*Los Angeles. Hollywood. 1977.* Crazy how a world so exciting, that drew me like a promise of freedom, would turn so dark so quickly.

* * *

My name is Marshall James. There's a Franklin in the middle, but I don't like it and I've never used it. I think my old man called me Franklin a couple times when he was pissed at me. Hildren James was an angry sonofabith. It gave him an excuse to drink, or at least another one in a long list of them. I remember him saying, "Franklin James, you get over here right now!" I got over there, too, wherever that was. It usually just meant placing myself within arm's length. It made it easier for him to slap me from a sitting position. He slapped us a lot, even my mom. He never hit her full on, as far as I recall, but being slapped across the face or on the top of the head was enough. She was diagnosed with breast cancer when I was sixteen and got the hell off the planet three months later. Who could blame her?

It was a long time ago. Everything at my age feels that

way. Time isn't really a *thing*. It doesn't pass. It doesn't fly, it doesn't crawl, it doesn't wait for anyone because it doesn't *wait* at all. It's more like something we spend our lives inside without realizing it, the way a fish spends its life in water. And, like water in a cracked fish tank, it drains away slowly.

I've got a manfriend who stays three nights a week with me in this crappy studio apartment within spitting distance of the bus terminal. His name is Buford McGibbon, but he goes by Boo. You would, too, if you'd been burdened with an antebellum name like that. It even sounds Confederate, but it's not. Boo's from upstate New York. He's also ten years younger than me, but not in any way the object of this older man's predation. We met when he took one of the tours I give for a living. If you spend much time in New York City you'll see people like me, leading groups of straggling tourists and a few curious locals around Greenwich Village or the bars in Brooklyn, reciting history and color commentary. My specialty now is the Gotham Ghost Land Tour. It offers several different routes in Manhattan, since people tend to die anywhere. It's not like the Bob Dylan Smoked a Joint Here tour—*Oh look, that's the window Joan Baez was gazing out when she wrote Diamonds and Rust*—or the Edgar Allen Poe tour I did for a while that made exactly one mention of Poe.

I remember Boo very well that first time we met. It was a History of Gay New York tour (I've done them all). The group consisted of wide-eyed queens from faraway ghettos, dykes, a few straight couples, several German speakers, and Boo. He was thirty-eight then, alone, hot as a griddle, lingering when the others melted away at the end. He was one of the few who tipped me. I remember taking the five dollar bill from him, saying thanks, and keeping hold of his hand longer than is proper for a tour guide, unless he's meeting the next love of his life in a moment of ridiculous serendipity.

We're an odd couple by today's gay standards. We're not married and have no plans to be. We'd rather have herpes than children. We don't live together. He has an apartment in Brooklyn and I'm in Hell's Kitchen, and we like it this way. We still have sex, which is saying something after a decade, but mostly we love each other in a very relaxed way. He knows I could die if the cancer comes back, and I know he'll miss me terribly. That's enough for now.

The other entity I allow into my life is a cat named Critter. He's four years old, which I know because I remember Justine taking him in as a kitten, as if a junkie prostitute had the wherewithal to take care of a cat. She lived across the hall from me and she asked me to feed him a few times when she was out of town. I had no idea where she went and she never told me. Then one day, about a year after she took Critter in, I got a knock at the door from Javier, our building super.

"You want a cat?" he asked me.

Javier speaking was a rare and curious thing.

"Where's Justine?" I said, as he stood in my doorway holding an animal that wanted nothing more than to be free from his clutches.

"She died," he said. Very matter-of-factly, as if she'd been a storefront that was open one day and closed the next.

"You know how she died?" I asked. Part of me dreaded being told she'd been strangled by a john.

"OD," he said, then shrugged: these things happen.

"Well," I replied, "we can't say that's a surprise, now, can we?"

I took the cat from his arms, and he's been living with me ever since.

That's my life: I'm a tour guide with no aspirations to be more. I'm a cancer survivor with one functioning lung. I've got a manfriend who spends a few nights a week with me and a cat that never leaves. And I've got stories to tell.

You see how things come around? I'm a man on borrowed time. We all are, but the debt collector announced his arrival in my case. I've outfoxed the bastard and outlived the expectations, and I started thinking, maybe I should tell people about those murders. The ones I was part of in Hollywood back then. Not murders I *participated* in, of course. This is not a deathbed confession. But I was part of it … *them* … and I figured I should go ahead and talk about it while I can. Some of the people involved are dead, and some of us are alive. I'm still not sure who the lucky ones are.

Now let's head over to the time machine. Strap yourself in, it all happens very quickly. I'll set the dial to 1977, the GPS to a town in Indiana where a lonely kid prepares his escape to Hollywood, the final destination a dive bar called the Paisley Parrot. Gay, mobbed up, a place for drunks, hustlers and dope dealers. My kind of bar.

# ONE

DRIVING CROSS COUNTRY IS A great way to experience America, provided you only do it once. That's how I got from Indiana to California within a week after graduating high school. There'd been nothing to keep me there. Mom had been dead almost three years. My younger brother and sister could take care of themselves. It wasn't hard to do with a father who asked very little of them except to keep the volume down on their bedroom stereos, not bring any venereal diseases home, and leave him alone at night to enjoy his drinking undisturbed.

I'd barely made it through school. By my senior year I was smoking so much pot it hovered around me in a cloud, like Pig-Pen from the Peanuts cartoon with his travelling dust devil. I knew it was a way of protecting myself—settling into a cocoon of marijuana, pills and booze so I didn't have to interact with anyone, or be hurt by them. I wouldn't admit it then, but I was a sensitive kid. It's hard not to be a little messed up when you've watched your mother die and your father respond by immersing himself in rum, all when you're a teenager who knows he's gay but isn't quite sure what that means. I knew it meant I liked guys—I'd known that since I was about five. I did not, however, have a gay identity. I didn't think about civil rights, or equality, or defending myself by insisting I was born this way. All I knew at eighteen was that I longed for a man I was never going to find in Elkhart, Indiana; my dad was hopeless, my mom was dead, my sister and brother lived in their own worlds as completely as I did. It was time to get the hell out.

Two days after a graduation ceremony I remembered as a patchy blackout, I loaded up my orange Gremlin, the one with the stains on the roof from popping all those beer cans in the front seat, and I pulled out of my parents' driveway without so much as a glance in the rearview mirror. I'd be back, but only in a taxi, and only for a few days every couple years. I wanted to get as far away from that house as I could while still being on the continent. Los Angeles, swimming pools, porn stars, here I come.

* * *

I remember listening to cassettes of Elton John's *Madman Across the Water* and David Bowie's *Young Americans* over and over as I drove from state to state. I spent a total of three nights in hotels, feeling very grown up paying for my own room, ordering drinks from room service because they didn't ask my age.

Anita Bryant was making headlines that year, trying to stop people like me from being teachers in California. The air was tense, the nightly news filled with conflict and division. Nothing's changed.

I finally arrived in Hollywood, unaware it was a neighborhood and not just a state of mind. It was late June, 1977. Jimmy Carter had not yet failed America's expectations of him. *Star Wars* was taking the country by storm trooper, and Marshall James was just about to create a new life for himself—young and thin, sexually deprived and determined to do something about it.

I had arrived in Mecca.

The Holy Land would soon reveal its seedy underclass of hustlers, chicken hawks, junkies, speed freaks and every manner of sexual predator. What saved me, I think, is that I was not easy prey. I learned the various rules of the various games and mastered them, all with open eyes and a gift for deal making: I was never taken advantage of, never a victim. I knew very well I could end up dead if I didn't stay strong and alert.

I had no idea, as 1977 came to an end and I paid my first month's rent on a small single apartment not far from the

Hollywood Bowl, that death was looking at all of us from the horizon, calculating its next move. Then, with the indifference of a river slowly rising over its banks,
death came to take us one by one.

# TWO

I'D BEEN IN L.A. FOR six years by the time it all began. That's an eternity in the life of a twenty-something. I'm not even sure I felt like a man yet. Part of me wanted to stay eighteen forever, but leaving home for Hollywood with absolutely no plan has a way of making you grow up quickly. It definitely exposed me to my own naiveté. When I'd left Indiana I had thought of myself as experienced and hardened. I'd come out as gay my junior year in high school, a very uncommon thing to do in the 1970s. I'd had a half dozen sexual experiences, a few so amazing I still remember them, the rest just quick encounters in McNaughton Park. (This was forty years before hookup apps, when you went to a park or a rest top on the highway to get your rocks off.)

Looking back on it, it was a deluded way to think. There are things an Indiana teenager simply cannot know or experience that he will find in ready supply on the streets of Hollywood. It was as if they were waiting for me—the men, the drugs, the sex. As if they had saved a place for me, until finally I arrived in my orange Gremlin and my tattered jeans and said, "I'm here, boys, take me as I am!" And they did.

I had just $200 in my wallet when I got off the Ventura Freeway and drove into Hollywood. I didn't know where I was. I had prepared some maps of the interstates and of Los Angeles itself, so I could find my way around. I knew from the *60 Minutes* piece that the Gold Cup was at the corner of Hollywood Boulevard and Las Palmas, so that's where I headed.

The Gold Cup was nearing the end of its run when I got there. It had opened in 1962 and was finally shut down by an LAPD task force for drugs and prostitution, which were plentiful at the coffee shop. I didn't know the place was doomed when I walked in, although it always felt that way.

Many of its customers had died from drug overdoses or disappeared into the great void of the sex trade. Boy prostitutes, girl prostitutes, pimps, johns and junkies. I fit right in.

I wasn't low on cash for long. I lived to tell about it, and if you had any knowledge of that life, you knew it was a tossup as to which one would take me out first—hustling or AIDS. I could have been strangled by a john who decided killing me was easier than paying me, but I also could have been given the kiss of death that had just started making the rounds when I showed up. It wouldn't reveal itself for a few more years but it was among us, silently passing man to man, leaving its deadly seeds to blossom and flower on our faces.

* * *

I met Butch Reardon six months after arriving in Hollywood. I'd been sleeping at the Hollywood Spa on Ivar when I wasn't crashed on a friend's couch. For $10 a night I got a skinny mattress in a narrow room and all the sex I wanted, plus some I didn't. My friends consisted mostly of other young men who called themselves escorts but who usually found their business by sticking their thumbs out on Santa Monica Boulevard. A casual drive down the thoroughfare offered dozens of hitchhikers eager to take any ride you paid them for. The Spa had opened three years earlier and was a popular spot for men seeking men at any hour of the day. Hustling on the premises was frowned upon but everyone knew it went on. We had to pay for the room somehow, and as long as nobody got arrested the owners looked the other way.

Butch's full name was Barton Samuel Reardon. He told me they started calling him Butch when he was a kid and he'd get a crew cut every summer, which the locals in his town called a 'butch.' By the time he stood in my doorway at the spa he'd made the butch cut permanent, but I'll admit it wasn't his haircut that got my attention.

That's how it started out with Butch—a couple hours of body contact followed by a night of talking. It was last time we had sex, but the beginning of a friendship that makes me smile to this day. Butch was a good guy. Butch was generous and kind. Butch looked after this stupid kid from the Midwest and made sure I stood a chance in the big, bad world of Los Angeles.

* * *

I moved in with Butch a week later. Sometimes we just know what shape a relationship should take. He was great in the sack, but I knew that first night he was much more valuable as a friend.

He had a two-bedroom apartment on Gower that he shared with a cat named Lurline. I moved into the second bedroom he used as an office and slept on a foldout sofa he had for guests. I'd only meant to be there a few days, but two years later I finally got my own place, a small apartment on Highland you could tour by turning in a circle and feigning amazement. *What a great apartment, Marshall! Lucky you!* It had a Murphy bed in one wall, a kitchen big enough for a table and two chairs, and a single window that looked out on a parking lot. By then I was working at the Dildo Factory and could afford the $275 a month in rent.

The Dildo Factory was my first real job in Hollywood, and one I managed to keep for four years. Its real name was Products Unlimited, a deliberately vague name chosen by the woman who owned it to keep the authorities away. We made and distributed wholesale sex toys, jells, harnesses and inflatable dolls, to sex shops across the country. There was even one in Elkhart, Indiana. We called it the Dildo Factory for obvious reasons. I was the assistant bookkeeper, hired off a smile and a smooth interview without any experience. God bless Gertie—she was the owner. Gertie Levy. An old, free love Jew who knew how to make a buck from lust. Her favorite sales were cash from local shops, which she would take and stuff in safe deposit boxes away from the prying eyes of the IRS.

Everything seemed perfect to me then. I had my own place. I hadn't turned a trick in years. Butch was still there for me, mentoring me in his way. I had a few friends who didn't spend their nights looking for johns. Life was good.

Butch and I toasted the New Year together, 1983. It was just the two of us in my apartment. Neither of us were fond of crowds and we'd skipped the usual party invitations. There was just some reason we wanted to be alone that night. It was only later I looked back on it and knew that forces were at work in our lives. I don't believe in God, but I believe in strangeness, in a cosmos that operates in ways beyond our understanding. Quantum physics, maybe. Parallel universes where all our disappointments never happened and there is no loss.

That New Year's Eve with Butch was a turning point. I told him I was leaving the Dildo Factory.

"I thought you liked it there," he said, lighting a cigarette while we waited for the final New Year's countdown.

"I'll never make good money with them," I replied. "And I don't want to work in a glorified sex warehouse the rest of my life. I'm twenty-five now."

"All grown up at last." He smiled at me and blew a cloud of smoke into the air. "So what are you going to do instead?"

I was excited to tell him. I'd been going to bartending school on weekends and I'd received my Certificate of Passage the previous Saturday.

"I'm going to be a bartender. I passed my exam!"

Butch hadn't known about the classes. I'd told myself I wanted to surprise him, but really I just didn't want his opinion until it was too late to dissuade me.

He looked at me, scrunching his face. "You and booze don't go so well together," he said. "Are you sure it's a good idea?"

He'd known me to drink too much on occasion and had expressed concern. I bristled at it that night, taking it as a lack of enthusiasm for my goals.

"What does that have to do with making bartending my profession? I hardly have sex anymore and I work at a dildo factory. It can be done."

"That's a good point."

I could tell he was unconvinced. My father had died an alcoholic and the statistics didn't favor me.

"So do you have a job in this new career yet?" he asked.

"I do, as a matter of fact."

I glanced at the small TV on a milk crate I had against a wall. Midnight was almost upon us and the partygoers were preparing to count backward.

"I'm going to work at the Paisley Parrot," I said. "I'm starting as a barback, but I know I can move up in six months, maybe less."

His silence was telling.

"The *Paisley Parrot*?" he said, as if he hadn't heard me correctly. He saw my reaction and quickly smiled. "That's great, Marshall, really. I'm happy for you."

He was not happy for me. The Paisley Parrot was a bar for people who drank themselves into oblivion and staggered home with someone they wouldn't remember meeting in the morning.

I was young. I didn't care what Butch thought of me working at the Parrot. I was thrilled to have something I could call a career, and to be leaving the Joy Jelly and sex toys behind.

Butch had a coughing fit, which I attributed to the Marlboros. The coughing subsided. The countdown began. *Ten, nine, eight, seven …*

It was the last carefree New Year's eve of our lives, mine and Butch's. It was the *before,* and everything that came later was the *after*. We didn't know it then. We toasted, we laughed, we smoked, we said goodbye as a new year came barreling at us, catching us unprepared.

# THREE

THE PAISLEY PARROT WAS EXACTLY the kind of bar I liked to drink in, especially when my love affair with alcohol was still mutual. I'd started with vodka and gin when I was in high school, courtesy of my dad's basement bar. It never closed, and it never ran dry. By the time I put on a cap and gown for my high school graduation and stumbled to the podium for my diploma, I'd been a hard drinker for several years. I'm not an alcoholic—I know how that sounds, most alcoholics deny what they are—but I was as close to being a lush as a teenager can be without running for the nearest rehab. For some reason my drinking didn't get worse, and I had it fairly under control by the time I decided to work in a bar.

I'd been going to the Parrot and places like it since I'd first moved to Hollywood. I've always thought it was because I was an Indiana kid. My identity was well formed before I got to L.A. and was exposed to the prevailing gay archetypes of the time—muscle boys, drama queens, and older men who'd been part of the scene so long they were cultural furniture. I'm not knocking it. I just knew who Marshall James was and I've stayed that way pretty much all my life.

I took pride in living in Hollywood, a neighborhood as diverse as it was seedy. There were black people in my apartment building, drag queens, straight couples, and, twice during my years living there, dead bodies. A woman on the sixth floor was found hanging from her shower curtain, self-inflicted; and a young man, a hustler I knew from my first year on the streets, was found on the fire escape with a syringe in his arm.

My haunts were close by. I liked bars where people went to drink, not to compare abs and gossip about their ex-boyfriends. Bars where they paid more attention to the glass of whiskey in front of them than to the guy who just walked through the door in torn jeans. There were several of them within walking distance: The Vine, on Vine Street, of course; LuLu's for the dykes; the 12 O'clock Lounge, named long ago for reasons forgotten; the Red River, where the banks overflowed with booze and the tears of failed ambition, and the Paisley Parrot, located discreetly near the corner of Fountain and Las Palmas. There was a neon parrot on the door but no name. The Parrot had been around since the late 1950s, a time when bars that catered to homosexuals did not announce themselves. The front window was tinted so dark you couldn't see inside even if all the lights were on. A recessed door opened onto a heavy curtain separating the world out there from the world in the Parrot. It served to protect them from each other: the people on the outside did not want to know what went on in there, and the patrons in the bar wanted no reminders that the world outside was waiting for them after the blackout, after the sloppy sex, after their best efforts to drink it all away.

I found the Parrot by accident. It wasn't really a hustler bar. The mob still ran it in the 1980s, but quietly, and they didn't want the attention cops brought with them. Being gay wasn't illegal anymore, but prostitution and its emaciated sister, drug sales, were very much against the law. The two went hand in hand. Most of the hustlers I'd known either traded their bodies for dope or had some to sell. If not, they knew someone, who was conveniently located in a dark corner of the bar or waiting in the back alley.

The criminal enterprise then holding sway in the greater Los Angeles area was the Bianchi family, reported to be an offshoot of the Brooklyn Bianchi mafia clan. Rumor had it the Brooklyn branch had been crippled by law enforcement and had expanded—or escaped—to the West Coast.

Fat Dick Montagano, the Bianchi family lieutenant who kept the bars in line and the cash flowing, only tolerated hustlers who gave him free blowjobs, so the pros stayed away. His name was Richard Montagano. Everybody called him Fat Dick behind his back because he'd once topped off at three hundred pounds, though he'd lost a third of it by the time I met him. I assumed he'd been stuck with the name as a kid, or maybe his mob bosses gave it to him. It wasn't a name anyone who valued their life would call him to his face, and we all knew to refer to him as Mr. Montagano when we addressed him or he was within earshot. If he overheard you, you might find a piece of piano wire embedded in your neck, so we left the name calling to people he was afraid of, who were all named Bianchi.

The mob presence in Los Angeles was once very powerful. After all, they'd founded Las Vegas, which was only four hours away in good traffic. But by the time I walked into the Parrot, they'd been reduced to pimping, moving drugs in from Mexico for domestic distribution, bookmaking, various other misadventures, and a few gay bars. Gregory Bianchi, the old guy who was the titular head of the family, had not been seen in public for several years and was rumored to be buried in the desert, his reputation used by his son and successor Anthony to instill fear in people's hearts. Other than that, I knew nothing about them and made no attempt to find out. It was enough just dealing with Fat Dick coming into the Parrot every Wednesday night to siphon off the Bianchis' take from the week's receipts. He was often accompanied by one pretty boy or another. He was married with three kids, but his taste for young male flesh was evident. It was also something you pretended not to notice. I'd been told he kept an apartment on Franklin Avenue for mob business on nights he didn't return to his family in Encino. I imagine a few of those pretty boys spent the evening there.

I'll admit to having the hots for the Parrot's bartender, Phil Seaton. He was the real reason I went to the Parrot a second time. I had other choices for bars, but none of them had Phil slinging drinks. He was thirty-ish, shaved head, tattoos on biceps exposed by a vest with no shirt. He had big hands. Some myths never die, and some are even true.

It had been two years between the time I first walked into the Paisley Parrot and the time I started working there. Phil had been there for eight years or so and had no plans to improve his situation. Like me, the Parrot was his kind of bar. And it turned out I was his kind of twenty-something. We started having sex a week after I ordered my first bourbon and Coke, sitting on a stool staring at his arms. That lasted about three months. It also caused friction between me and Butch. Not because Butch was jealous, but because he believed Phil was a bad influence. I told him Phil and I only did lines of cocaine, washed down with two or three drinks. We stayed away from the crystal meth that was starting to be popular, and I would never use a syringe. But Butch worried and he warned. I ignored it, had a great run with Phil, and let it fall by the wayside. Phil met another young guy a month after we stopped playing together and neither of us made anything of it.

Those first years in L.A. flew quickly. I remember my twenty-fifth birthday, how old I felt and how fast I thought my life was passing. It's an easy thing to think at that age. I look back now and marvel at how young twenty-five is, and how foolish.

I'd celebrated that New Year's Eve with Butch, unaware of the darkness ahead. I'd seen him out just after midnight, then headed to the Paisley Parrot for my first drink of 1983. Phil was there with a few of the regulars. He set me up with my usual, a shot of Jim Beam in a glass of Coke. I bought the house a round, and one more time we toasted in the dying light.

# FOUR

DAVID BOWIE'S *LET'S DANCE* WAS a monster hit that year. So was Eurythmics' *Sweet Dreams,* and Sting's *Every Breath You Take,* a meditation on stalking that got reimagined by the public as a love song. The space shuttle Challenger made its maiden voyage with the first woman astronaut, Sally Ride, among the crew, and the CDC warned blood banks of a possible problem with the blood supply.

The Redskins won the Super Bowl, the Orioles won the World Series, and the domestic AIDS death toll was a mere 2,304 for the year.

President Ronald Reagan had still not said the word 'AIDS.'

Is it any wonder so many of us sought companionship and distraction in the bars? The worst had yet to come our way, but we'd already grown accustomed to seeing … or, rather, *not seeing* … friends at our favorite watering holes as they vanished like fireflies in the night. There was a nervousness to every arrival, walking into the Screw or the Gold Dust or the Paisley Parrot, looking quickly around to identify faces we knew. It brought relief to see familiar faces, another nightly reprieve from our slow, steady extinction.

I was a happy guy the first few months on the job, starting as a barback with Phil. The Parrot was a great place to learn the trade. It was a slower, drunker kind of establishment. It wasn't like Whistles or The Omega, where a bartender could lose five pounds in a night running back and forth along the bar filling drinks for trendsetters. The Parrot was reserved and quiet, more of a gentleman's bar, if the gentleman was inebriated and gawking at anyone under forty. We had a TV along the wall that showed muted MTV videos all night while music came from a jukebox by the bathroom. It was easy to stroll back and forth along the bar for an entire shift—no rush, no frantic calling out for cocktails. Just a couple dozen regulars whose drinks we knew as well as we knew their names. There was Bobby Bray, early 50s, who'd run his own bar for twenty years until he went bankrupt buying into a pyramid scheme. There was Quincy, a retired drag queen who always came in with a protégé or two in their 20s. There was Jude and Lester, Maryanne, Gilda and a dozen more. I knew the songs each of them would play on the jukebox and when to cut them off from the vodka or rum. Even a mob bar has standards; by the time a customer is ordering another shot from the floor, you've got an obligation to say no.

You could still smoke in bars then, and working there was a little grimy slice of heaven for me: I could go through a pack of Marlboros in a single shift and put back three or four shots of anything I wanted, always at the expense of an admiring customer. My drinking had picked up slightly, not surprising given the environment. It's hard to imagine a better work life for the man I was at twenty-five. I'd even get lucky sometimes and take someone home.

One of those guys I got lucky with changed everything. His name was Bentley Wennig, an unusual name unless your father's a car enthusiast. He went by Ben—who wouldn't with a name like that? He'd gotten lost and wandered into the Parrot to ask for directions. It was a Wednesday night, which meant Fat Dick was there to take the Bianchi family skim for the week. Dick's reaction was how I knew Ben had walked in: the scary mob lieutenant couldn't stop staring at the young man who'd just appeared through the curtain.

Even Phil did a double-take, and he was as jaded as they came. Another handsome face, even one as startling as Ben's, did not usually merit a stare from Phil. Maybe it was the surprise of seeing someone as clean cut as Ben walking into a bar as dirty minded as the Parrot.

"Can I help you?" I said. I'd been working the bar with Phil for two weeks, having been promoted to bartender under his training. I would normally say, "What'll you have?", but this guy looked lost. I wasn't even sure he was gay.

He walked up to the bar, each step increasing my heart rate. I felt myself getting hard and was glad to be behind the bar.

Ben had dark brown hair just long enough to tickle the tops of his ears. He was clean shaven, no stubble, exposing perfect skin the color of cream. His eyes were so deep and liquid brown I thought of chocolate melting in front of me. And then he smiled …

"I'm kind of lost," he said. He looked around, trying to form an impression of the bar.

"Hmm," I said, smiling back. "How does someone get 'kind of' lost?"

"Well," he said, dipping his head in a show of embarrassment, "I was supposed to meet a friend at a bar on the corner of Santa Monica and Las Palmas. I'm new in town, like, two days."

"It would help if you were on Santa Monica," Phil said.

I jumped. I hadn't noticed Phil come up behind me. He slipped a coaster and a napkin in front of the stranger. Was he poaching on my territory?

"You're two blocks away," said Phil. "You're looking for LuLu's Bar None. Is your friend a lesbian?"

"Yeah," the man said. "Best friends since high school. She's the reason I moved here." Then, looking at me longer than a typical customer would, he added, "Well, one of them." He glanced at his watch. "I'm early anyway, I might as well have something. Vodka rocks?"

"Marshall here will take care of you." Phil winked at me and headed down the bar to refill one of the regulars.

"I'm Marshall," I said, as I set about making his drink.

"Ben," he replied, extending his hand. Few people shake hands with bartenders, that's not why we're there. The gesture amused me, so I shook his hand, noticing a beautiful gold ring with a striking green stone on his right pinky.

"Jade?" I asked.

He glanced at the ring, easing his hand away. "Oh, yes, from my grandmother for my last birthday. I can always count on Granny to find perfect gifts."

It was only later, when Ben was wiping sweat off his chest with a hand towel, that I learned his full name was Bentley. He was twenty-seven years old. He'd moved to L.A. that very week from Bellevue, Washington. The only person he knew in town was Becky Walters, his dyke friend we'd said goodbye to after a 3:00 a.m. breakfast at the Buffalo Diner before heading to my place.

Is love possible after just one orgasm? I don't know, so to be safe we made it three. By the time Ben left my apartment, the sun was well above the horizon and I was as sure as I have ever been that happiness had called my name.

# FIVE

WE DIDN'T HAVE SMART PHONES in 1983. When you wanted to reach someone, you used this thing called a telephone. It came with a cord stuck into a wall and numbered buttons you had to push. There were even a few rotary phones still around with confounding circular disks that had finger holes in them. When you picked up the headset you heard a dial tone, then you called the person you were trying to contact and either talked to them or left a message on another contraption called an answering machine.

I tried reaching Ben several times over the next few days. He wasn't avoiding me, he was just very busy. Your first week in a big city is consumed with deciding what you'll do for a living and the other thousand details of rearranging a life. I left a message on Ben's answering machine. He left one on mine. Back and forth. We managed to speak once, on Sunday night when I was pulling my first solo shift at the Parrot. Phil's mother had broken her leg in a fall and he'd gone to Bakersfield that weekend to help her. Normally it was just me and Phil working nights with one of the barbacks for support. If we needed help behind the bar we called Derek or Freeze. They were the part-timers and our backup. When Phil asked if I wanted one of them to help me, I said no, I can do this, and found myself nearly overwhelmed. A dozen serious drinkers on a Sunday night can be very demanding. So when Ben called the bar around 10:00 p.m., I didn't think anything of telling him I'd speak to him in the morning.

"I really want to see you again," he'd said quickly. "I've just been so busy."

"I get it," I'd replied. The phone was cradled between my ear and my shoulder as I hurried to fill another drink order. "I can't wait to see you, too. Let's talk tomorrow and make this happen."

I don't remember anything from the rest of my shift. When you're that harried, time not only flies, but blurs. I made it through. I cut off the drunks who'd had too many, which was a high percentage of the Parrot's clientele. I'd fended off three passes made by men who wouldn't remember making them the next day. I shared the workload with Brandon, the new barback who'd been hired to replace me in that position. And I'd made enough in tips to confirm my belief that bartending was a good career choice. It all depends on what you want in life, and at that point I didn't have many wants: a one-bedroom apartment as soon as I could afford it, a new used car to replace the ailing Gremlin, some nice clothes and a stereo. That was pretty much my wish list … oh, and a good man. I was twenty-five. I felt time passing, and I thought I was ready to settle down for a while. The longest relationship I'd had was three months, ending in more of a shrug than a heartache. There was Butch, of course, and my short-lived fling with Phil the bartender. But nothing I would classify as a relationship. Remembering the phone call with Ben when I was cashing out for the night, I had the crazy idea he might be the one to change that. There was just something about the guy, and as I twist-tied the two big trash bags collected every night behind the bar, I found myself wishing I'd stopped what I was doing and talked to him when he'd called. I've never liked unfinished conversations, then or now.

There was an alley behind the Paisley Parrot. It's still there as far as I know—alleys don't tend to move—but the Parrot is long gone, replaced by a succession of retail shops, nail salons and, as of this writing, a pet store. I suppose the dumpsters are still there, too. Technology hasn't done much to improve trash disposal.

I always took the bags out one at a time, since they were so heavy. Brandon had gone home with my encouragement. The kid was exhausted from working and I was used to closing the place down myself, even when Phil was on duty. I propped the back door open with a brick we used for that purpose, and lugged the giant brown plastic bag over to the dumpster.

The lids were closed in a feeble effort to keep the rats out and the smells in. I set the bag down a moment, pushed up the large metal lid of the dumpster, and found myself staring into the face of a corpse.

And not just any corpse. It was the dead, broken body of the young man I hadn't had time to talk to that evening. The man whose smile had sent me back on my heels when he'd walked into the bar less than a week ago. The man I'd fantasized ten minutes earlier about calling my boyfriend.

Those astonishing brown eyes were open, dead and lifeless. Something was wrapped around his neck, dug so deeply into his flesh I didn't recognize at first what it was. His right hand rested over his chest, as if pledging allegiance to a dark lord. Something about it struck me, a fleeting detail, but the thought vanished in the shock of the scene. There was no light in his beautiful gaze, only a darkness he'd seen in his final moments that was about to make its way into our lives.

# SIX

I HAD THE WORST DRY heaves of my life, puking with nothing coming out but gasps, water and spit. By the time the cops showed up, my abdomen ached from convulsing and I'd been squatting outside the bar's back door for fifteen minutes. Once I saw Ben's body in the dumpster, I let the lid crash down over him and ran back inside to call the police. It's hard to imagine a time when there were no cell phones—I couldn't call 911 from the side of the dumpster while I stared at the dead body of a man I knew. I couldn't take pictures, either, which is a good thing, given how quick we are now to turn everything into a snapshot. I had to live with it, to *be there* in those minutes while I waited for help. I wanted to go back to the dumpster, to open it and see him. *Was he really dead*? I'd assumed he was, but I had not checked for a pulse or shaken him to see if he would wake up, if *we* would wake up, from this nightmare. He looked dead, that was for damn sure. His face was blue and there was what looked like a phone cord tightened around his neck. He had to be dead, didn't he?

Finally I heard a siren and knew it was the one sent to answer my cry. I'd screamed into the phone, "I need someone! My friend's dead … in a dumpster!"

"Try to be calm," the dispatcher had said. "Why do you think your friend is dead?"

"Because he's *blue*!" I'd shouted. "He's blue and his eyes are open and he's got, like, a phone cord or something around his neck … in a *dumpster*!"

"Can you tell me where this dumpster is?"

She was so calm. I knew that was her job. She wouldn't last long if she let herself get caught up in the terror and anger she must have heard every night taking emergency calls.

"The Paisley Parrot," I said. "Behind the building. I'm the bartender."

"The fag bar on Las Palmas?"

Her words made me pause for only an instant. Back then people still said 'fag' easily and without repercussion, often without offense. Other than that one word, she'd been very professional.

"That's it, yes," I said.

"I'll send a patrol car. Don't leave, please. What was your name?"

"Marshall," I said, feeling immense fatigue come over me as the adrenaline rush began to fade. "Marshall James."

"Marshall, just stay put. An officer will be there very soon."

Her idea of 'very soon' was my idea of forever. I went back outside, crouched down by the door, and started to vomit air.

* * *

I knew I was a suspect from the way the cop questioned me. I couldn't fault him for it. You wouldn't have to be a clever killer to throw a body in a trash container and call the police screaming that you'd discovered it. What I did fault him for was his dismissive attitude that only got sharper once he realized this was *the* Paisley Parrot, or, as the dispatcher had so matter-of-factly called it, the fag bar.

The lead cop introduced himself as Officer Haggerty. That's all the information he gave me about himself. The cruiser had shown up with two policemen in it. No ambulance came with them—I suppose they weren't willing to take the word of a hysterical man in the middle of the night claiming there was a dead body in the trash. They wanted to verify it first, which they did within a minute after arriving. Haggerty's partner, a ridiculously muscled black man whose name I'll never know, went to check out the scene while Haggerty questioned me, standing between me and the dumpster as if he wanted to keep me from seeing what was going on.

"Victim in the trash," the black cop said, calling out over his shoulder. "Looks like we've got a homicide here, Sid."

I now knew Haggerty's first name, which seemed incongruous to me at the time. He didn't look like a Sid, more like a Dave or a Frank. I remember thinking this as his posture changed with the confirmation of Ben's corpse just ten feet behind him, as if I had suddenly become armed and dangerous. The only thing I was armed with was a handful of paper towels I'd grabbed when the puking started.

"That your boyfriend?" Haggerty asked me, offering up an amused snarl.

"He was a friend," I said. "His name is ... was ... Bentley Wennig. Ben."

"Must have pissed you off pretty bad."

"I didn't kill him," I said. My shock and fear had turned to anger. "I found him like that, asshole."

There are times in our lives when we know what we've just said was stupid and possibly life threatening. That was one of those times for me. I knew from the hardness of his expression he might arrest me, or just beat the crap out of me. He did neither.

"I'll have to ask you to sit in the car," he said. "This is going to take a while."

He led me over to the cruiser and opened the back door. I complied, my mind racing between grief, fear, and calculation as it dawned on me that I did not have the upper hand in this situation.

"I'm going to close the door," he said. "Just sit back and relax."

"Am I under arrest?" I asked.

"That's not my call."

He closed the door, leaving me in the back of the patrol car to watch while he began speaking into his shoulder mic. I knew at that moment there would be more of them—backup, crime scene technicians, all the people I imagined show up at a murder scene. I sat back and closed my eyes, replaying my last, short conversation with Ben over and over in my mind.

After what seemed like an eternity but had only been about ten minutes, I was startled from my thoughts by a knock at the window. My eyes had been shut all that time, despite hearing more vehicles arrive. There had been no more sirens. I looked up at the window and almost jumped.

Just outside, smiling slightly at me, was a man whose handsomeness seemed grotesquely inappropriate under the circumstances. Or maybe it was my appreciation of him that was inappropriate. How does one go from the despair of finding a dead body to the strange, erotic sensation of being stared at by a cop in a suit? He stepped back slightly and motioned for me to get out of the police car.

I did as he told me, closing the door behind me.

It was his eyes, I think. Even in the deepest night, as dawn crept toward us, their blueness was inescapable. The smile, while it had been fleeting and intended to disarm me, had flashed with a crookedness that intruded on my guilt and grief. He was slightly shorter than me, with brown hair that appeared purposely shaggy. He was wearing a dark blue suit, white shirt and blue tie with a brass tie clip. Who dressed like that at four in the morning?

"My name's Kevin McElroy," he said. "Mac to most people. I'm a detective from the Hollywood Division."

I had my answer.

"Marshall James," I replied. I extended my hand but he did not reciprocate. I don't know if that was some kind of technique to keep distance between himself and a witness, or if I was a suspect and familiarity was against protocol. What would have seemed rude to me any other time didn't bother me. I let my arm fall back to my side.

"Let's step over here," he said. He led me back toward the open door of the Parrot. I thought for a moment he was going to take me inside, but he stopped short of it. Positioning himself between me and the building, he forced me to face him, away from the activity going on behind us. A van had arrived. Yellow crime scene tape had been strung around the dumpster and along the area of the parking lot where it sat. There were two police cruisers, at least six people, and the detective who had me standing to the side while he took out a notebook and pen.

"Tell me exactly what happened," he said.

I opened my mouth and it all came tumbling out, about Ben, about the phone call, about finding him in the dumpster. I even found myself telling this man about my first five years in Los Angeles. He did his best to keep me focused, and several times he made me repeat myself, especially with details from that night. Who had been in the bar? What was the barback's name? Did I always close out alone?

He, too, asked me if Ben was my boyfriend, but his tone was gentle, not mocking or judgmental.

"No," I said, taking a deep breath. "Not yet anyway. And now he never will be."

My body gave out on me then. I began sobbing. I was so tired, so frightened, and so alone. But I would never be as alone as Ben, strangled and dropped in a dumpster behind a mobbed-up gay bar in the middle of the night.

## SEVEN

I SLEPT THAT NIGHT THE way you might if you had proof there were monsters under the bed. It was sleep in fits and starts, snatches of oblivion interrupted by spasms of memory: Ben in the dumpster, his eyes opened wide and dead; the phone cord embedded in his neck; the brief call we had that I paid so little attention to, not knowing it would be the last time we spoke.

*You didn't know him,* I told myself, troubled that I was so devastated by his death. Was it the loss of life, or the loss of a short-lived fantasy, or just the shock of it all that had shaken me so completely?

*He was a human being. You found him murdered and left in the garbage.* I raised my head and turned to the bedside clock: 6:00 a.m. The sun was almost up and I'd only been in bed two hours. I sat up and slid my feet around, letting them hit the floor. I could not go back to sleep, if I'd slept at all. Early morning light was spreading across the horizon. I could see the Hollywood sign from my window. To me it was just a bunch of letters stuck up on a hillside. Whatever allure it once held for me was lost in those early days of hustling and hoping; now it was more like the centerpiece of a spider's web, the shiny, succulent *thing* the cunning spider had wrapped and placed there while it waited for its next victim to come along.

I went into my kitchen that opened onto the living room, separated only by a door frame. I'd painted the frame a garish red, trying to add color to an otherwise unremarkable apartment. There was a pitcher of cold coffee waiting in the refrigerator—I've had a fondness for cold coffee since my teenage years. It doesn't make me wait for it to brew.

I was glad to have it that morning. I needed to wake up, and a cup of cold coffee with a splash of milk for flavor was just the thing. I had a mug of it, then made a refill and decided it was not too early to call Butch.

I was scheduled to see Detective McElroy in a few hours and I needed to talk to someone friendly first. I knew I would be a suspect by default. I also knew I had nothing to do with Ben's death and Butch was the person who could help me get my story straight.

*There's no story to get straight,* I corrected myself. *Just tell McElroy again exactly what happened. You spoke briefly to Ben on the phone. You closed out the bar alone, took the trash out, and there he was, waiting for you.*

Had he been waiting for me? Had he come to see me and stopped somewhere on the way? Had he met someone else in a town full of strangers and made the worst judgment call of his life?

My head was spinning. I sat on the couch, took a big swallow of cold coffee, and reached for the phone. Butch would know what to do.

* * *

Butch did not know what to do or what to say. He was stunned that the murder he'd seen reported on the morning news involved me. He was already up when I called. That should not have surprised me: most people didn't work in bars and get home at 3:00 a.m. Butch was a paralegal in a downtown law firm, so it was natural he'd be up early with the rest of the grunts. Working in an office required a shower, shave, and carefully chosen office drag to play the part from nine to five. Butch was good at the part, too. He rarely talked about his job and I never asked, assuming he would tell me anything he wanted me to know.

"What are you so worried about?" he said, as our conversation came to a close. We'd been on the phone for twenty minutes. I'd relived everything in detail, from Phil taking off to see his mother in Bakersfield to my finding Ben in the dumpster.

"I'm worried they'll think I did it."

"That's crazy."

"Yeah, well, the whole thing is crazy. What if they find my fingerprints?"

"On what, Marshall?"

"I don't know. His dick, maybe."

He ignored the comment. "Did you sleep at all? You're talking like someone who's been up all night."

"I slept on and off, mostly off."

"What time's your interview?"

"My interrogation, you mean?"

"Stop it! Your interview with the cop, when is it?"

"Ten a.m.," I said, tipping up my cup for the last drop of coffee. "Should I take a lawyer with me? I don't have one. You know lots of lawyers, what do you think?"

"I don't think you're at the lawyer stage yet," he said. "But if it sounds like he's accusing you, then stop talking and call me. In the meantime, rest a while. Take a shower. Eat breakfast. And just tell the guy what happened."

"I already did."

"So tell him again. You have nothing to fear."

"He's hot," I said, apropos of nothing.

"Oh for godsake. I have to go, really. Meet me for lunch at Crepe Stanley's, you can tell me how it went."

I'd told Butch several times I wasn't a crepe fan. My Hoosier insides weren't satisfied with mushrooms or fruit folded inside tissue paper. I also didn't care for the atmosphere at Crepe Stanley's, mostly lawyers, paralegals and bail bondsmen. There was a reason people called it *Creep* Stanley's. But it was a block from Butch's office so I said yes.

"I'll be there at noon," I said. "Assuming I'm not in a holding cell."

"You'll be fine, Marshall. Now just relax and eat something."

We hung up. His reminder to eat something set my stomach churning. I normally ate a light snack before bed when I got home, but I'd been too distraught to think about food last night.

I would do as Butch suggested. I'd take a shower, dress, and have some breakfast at a diner up the street before heading to Hollywood Division to tell the detective what I'd already told him in depressing detail.

# EIGHT

THE HOLLYWOOD POLICE STATION IS located on Wilcox Avenue near the corner of De Longpre. A lot of streets in L.A. are called avenues, I don't know why. (In New York City an avenue looks like an *avenue*—wide, filled with pedestrians jaywalking in every direction and cars doing their best to avoid them.) The red brick station building is squat and unassuming, as likely to be mistaken for a library branch as a police station.

I arrived a half hour early. I parked two blocks away on Fountain, preferring the walk to feeling cornered in the parking lot. Was I worried someone I knew would see me going in? Or maybe I thought if I left my car far enough away it would magically prevent me from being arrested. There was definitely something superstitious about the decision, as if going there was bad luck, which it proved to be for many people.

A police officer staffed the front desk. There was some activity, but not a flurry of it. It wasn't like the police stations I'd seen on television. It looked like a typical large front office, except it was filled with men and women in uniforms.

"Can I help you?" the officer asked when I approached the wide desk.

"I have an appointment."

"With who?"

"Detective Kevin McElroy."

He turned his attention to a computer screen. Computers then were bulky and looked like small TVs with dark green screens. I don't know if he was checking a calendar or a time log or exactly what he was looking at, but a moment later he turned back to me and said, "Have a seat."

There were sterile metal benches pressed against a wall,

as if comfort was the last thing on offer while you waited to give a statement or file a complaint. No coffee table, no magazines, no information pamphlets.

I took a seat and waited. It didn't take long. Detective McElroy was early, too, and came out ten minutes before our scheduled appointment.

"Mr. James," he said, extending his hand this time.

I stood and shook hands. His was warm and a little moist. I smiled and looked into his eyes, bluer and more piercing than they were the night before. Daylight can do that.

"Detective McElroy," I said, feeling my throat go dry. Was it from knowing I was about to be interrogated, or from the sensation of a warm palm on mine?

"Let's go into a back room."

He led the way, walking us past the front desk and along a hallway. Three doors down he turned into a small conference room. "Please," he said, "have a seat."

It wasn't what I'd expected. There was no single chair bolted to the floor. There was no iron ring for leg chains. There was no large mirror on the wall with someone behind it peering in and deciding if I was guilty based on my body language. There was no low-hanging overhead heat lamp to make me sweat, and the temperature was quite comfortable.

*It's a conference room,* I told myself. The only concession to TV drama was a tape recorder on the table.

He even pulled a chair out for me.

He wasn't wearing a jacket that day. I suppose you wouldn't when you're in your own office. His shirt was robin's egg blue, and he wore an unexpectedly festive tie that had a cartoon whale on it, fastened in place by an American flag tie pin.

"How are you this morning?" he asked, walking around the table and sitting across from me.

"I could use a good night's sleep," I said. My hands were trembling slightly so I clasped them together on the table.

"I bet. Finding someone in a dumpster can ruin your night, especially someone you knew."

"Barely," I said too quickly, instantly feeling like Peter in the Bible denying he'd known Jesus. Ben had been my friend for a few days. We'd had sex several times in our one night together, and I had cast him as a possible winner in my Dating Game fantasy. And there I was pushing him away to protect myself, depicting him as a stranger, or at most an acquaintance, whose body I'd found with the trash.

"How long you knew him doesn't change how it must have felt," he said, surprisingly gentle. "I've seen a lot of dead bodies in this job and it's never stopped ..."

I waited for him to finish the sentence.

"Hurting," he said, as if he'd searched for another word but not found one. "For the family, if there is one, and for the loss of life. The day I don't care is the day I won't do this anymore."

I remember cocking my head and looking at him. He was not what I'd expected. *This* was not what I'd expected.

"I'm going to turn the tape recorder on now," he said. He leaned up and reached for the recorder, pushing a button. "Please state your name for the record."

"Marshall Franklin James," I said, including my middle name. They would know what it was anyway, once they investigated me, which I knew they would.

"Where do you live, Marshall?"

"On Highland Avenue."

"The address, please."

And so it went for the next hour. Once I got my personal information out he began to ask me questions about the night before, beginning with when I got to work. I told him I'd only been a full-fledged bartender for a few weeks. I told him Phil had taken the night off when his mother got hurt. I told him I'd sent Brandon home after last call and was finishing up when I found Ben's body. It was such a strange, brutal thing to say: *Ben's body*. I wondered if there was some line we all cross when we go from being us to being corpses.

It's an uncomfortable truth.

* * *

Detective McElroy did not ask for my life's history; it wasn't germane at that point to a murder investigation. He didn't ask if I'd turned tricks on Santa Monica Boulevard or if I had cocaine hidden in my sock. He didn't ask me how old I was when I came out as gay, or if I ever had. For all he knew, I masqueraded as a straight man when I wasn't at the Parrot—lots of us did then and still do.

He kept all his questions specific to the time frame of the murder. I told him everything I could remember, up to and including his arrival on the scene last night.

"What did you know about Ben Wennig?" he asked sometime around the forty-five minute mark. I knew the time because I'd glanced at my watch. There was no clock in the room. *Like a casino*, I thought. *They don't want you to know how long you've been here.*

The question made me stop. What *did* I know about Ben? I knew he'd arrived in Los Angeles two days before he wandered into the Paisley Parrot. I knew he had a lesbian friend—did she know by now he was dead? Who would tell her?

I knew he wanted to be a screenwriter, along with ten thousand other people living in L.A. I knew he was an eager and enthusiastic lover, and he wore a jade ring on his right little finger. But not much else about him. We had not discussed our previous lives during the hours we'd spent together in my Murphy bed. It suddenly bothered me that I had not asked him meaningful questions when I'd had the chance. Had he really been new to the city, or was that the backstory to some elaborate reinvention? Maybe there was more to Ben than he'd let on. It occurred to me he might have been killed by someone he knew, for reasons shared only between him and his killer. What I truly knew about Ben amounted to *nothing*.

"Are you okay?" McElroy said, staring at me. I must have looked distressed, because he reached across the table and put his hand over mine.

*Oh, shit.*

"Would you like some water?"

"No, I'm fine," I lied. "I just got lost there for a second. Are we finished yet?"

Our hands were still touching.

"For now, yes," he said, leaning back and taking his hand with him.

That's when it hit me: the hand. What had bothered me about Ben's hand when I'd seen it lying against his chest in the dumpster.

"The ring was gone," I said.

"Excuse me?"

"He had a jade ring on his little finger, in a gold band. He said his grandmother gave it to him."

"You think whoever killed him took it?"

"I don't know what I think. I think I need to sleep. I think I need to eat."

"Fair enough, we can end the interview for now."

He turned off the tape recorder and looked at me. "If it eases your mind, I don't think you had anything to do with this, Mr. James."

"You don't?"

He smiled. "You don't seem like the body-in-a-dumpster type."

I hesitated. "What type do I seem like?"

He didn't answer. Instead he took a business card and pen from his shirt pocket.

"I'm going to give you my number," he said.

"Isn't it on the card?"

"My home number."

He wrote it down and slid the card across the table to me.

"In my experience people remember things after the fact, sometimes in flashes, or even a smell they encounter. It may happen for you, it may not, but if it does I want you to be able to reach me."

"Should I give you mine?" I asked, taking out my wallet and putting his card in the money holder.

"I have it."

I blushed: how stupid of me. "Of course you do. You also have my middle name and my exact address."

I was trying to be funny. He didn't laugh.

"One last thing," he said, standing from the table, a signal for me to do the same. "I want you to be careful."

"I don't understand."

"There's a killer out there," he said, a serious expression on his face. "A killer who was just outside the bar you were in. He may have even ordered a drink from you. Remember that."

It was the first time in the past twelve hours I'd considered this. Whoever killed Ben had put his body in the Parrot's dumpster while I was working there. *Had* he been in the bar? Had I served him a wine cooler or shot of tequila while he steeled himself for murder? *Did I know him*?

"Thank you for coming in," he said, opening the conference room door and holding it for me.

"My pleasure," I replied. Realizing how ridiculous it sounded, I added, "Bad choice of words, of course it wasn't. A man's dead. There was no pleasure in it at all, Detective McElroy."

"Mac."

"Pardon me?

"Call me Mac," he said. "Everyone does."

*Mac.* With the startling blue eyes and the warm hands.

I left the police station conflicted. I wanted never to return, but, strangely, I wanted to be questioned again, by Mac, a homicide detective investigating a murder with which I was now inextricably involved.

# NINE

CREPE STANLEY'S WAS LOCATED A block from the Superior Courthouse on Hill Street. It was a convenient location for the thousands of people employed in the city's legal industry, from trial lawyers to mailroom attendants. It was also an easy walk from the offices of Cryer & Dempsey, the law firm where Butch had worked as a paralegal for eight years. Butch had no interest in becoming an attorney and told me he was content with the level of success he'd achieved. He saw himself growing old doing what he was good at, collecting a pension (they still had them then), and maybe someday getting married to the man of his dreams.

"Married?" I'd said. "Gay people can't get married, that's crazy!"

It wasn't what he'd wanted to hear. He brushed off the comment, saying, "It could happen," then moved on to whatever else we spoke about that day.

I had never been inside Cryer & Dempsey. Butch was open about his sexuality with his colleagues, but he preferred meeting friends outside or in the lobby.

I'd left the police station in a minor state of confusion over the interview with Mac. *Was I really calling him 'Mac'? What was that about?* I knew what it was about: with an innocent touch of a hand I had superimposed Detective Kevin McElroy onto my dream-man template. Butch had been there once, as had Phil from the Parrot and, tragically, Ben before he was murdered. Others had been there in high school and a few after my move to Los Angeles, including one who insisted on paying me for an overnight stay when all we'd done was have dinner and talk about his estranged wife.

*Creep* Stanley's was inexplicably popular. It was run by woman named Pearl who'd named it after her late father. It was a touching detail but did nothing  to redeem the small restaurant with the line outside waiting for a flaccid, cheese-oozing crepe with a side of kale before anyone knew kale was a super food for the gullible. Today we would say it was *trending* and customers would snap photos of their food to auto-upload on Instagram. Back then it was more about networking and keeping to a tight lunch hour.

There were six tables inside and a counter with stools that ran along the front window. Wanting what we see other people eating is a big part of a restaurant's success. There was a lunch hour crowd outside waiting to get in, and there were a half dozen lucky ones already sitting on the stools eating crepes and looking super busy. It was the closest thing I ever saw in L.A. to the pointless frenzy of Manhattan.

I found Butch near the head of the line. He saw me walking up the street and waved me in front of twelve angry people who didn't care that I was with him; they saw someone cutting in front of a crowded line and would rather see me hit by a truck.

"Thanks for being on time," he said. "They're very strict at work with their definition of a lunch hour."

In the nearly six years I'd known Butch his office routine had not varied, except for how late he stayed. One of the peculiarities of his job was not being allowed any flexibility with his lunch hour, which ran precisely from 12:00 p.m. to 1:00 p.m. He never said what punishment they'd hand out if he showed up a minute late, maybe because it had never happened. He also never told me who in the office handed down that edict or why. It could have been the office manager Myra, who'd been given absolute power over the paralegals and interns. Or it could have been his immediate boss, a lawyer named Jarrod Garfield who Butch had described as handsome, married and sexually conflicted. Or it could have been old man Cryer himself, a throwback to the 1920s. Butch said little about the septuagenarian except that he got the feeling Cryer found him distasteful for some reason.

"Maybe he picked up on the gay thing," I said once.

"Yeah, and maybe he wants a little paralegal action with the door closed. Not gonna happen."

We finally made it inside Crepe Stanley's and were seated by a harried young woman dressed in the latest punk chic. All the tables were two-tops. It hastened the turnover.

No sooner had the punk chick handed us menus than her slightly taller clone glided up to take our order. I hadn't looked at the selections yet. Luckily Butch knew what he wanted and asked for the sausage crepes with goat cheese. I saved us time and said I'd have the same. She turned and fled, leaving the unread menus in our hands. I hated the place.

"Sausage and goat cheese?" I said. "I thought crepes were fruity French things."

"No," said Butch, nodding toward an unnaturally slim man sitting at a nearby table with a woman. "*He's* a fruity French thing."

We could make these jokes to each other in those days. We could say 'fag' and not be hounded from polite society. We wore colorful hankies to signal which side of the top/bottom equation we were on. The times were both freer and less free, much like today.

"So tell me about the interview," he said.

I imagined the room growing silent, which it did not. It was my self-consciousness flaring up. Could people hear me? Did it matter?

"He wants me," I said.

"What? Seriously?"

"Or I want him. Or we want each other. He touched my hand and sparks flew … or one spark anyway, straight to my dick, or my heart, I don't know. It was the strangest half hour I've spent in a very long time, if you don't count that guy who did himself with a shoe."

Butch laughed at that, and the laugh turned to a cough. The same cough I'd heard New Year's Eve, the cough he said was nothing but we both knew was something.

I waited for his fit to subside. "You've seen a doctor, yes?"

"It's on my list."

Seeing a doctor was on everybody's list, and most of us kept moving it down, past 'buy a new refrigerator' and 'arrange cremation.' Doctors' offices had become symbols of worse things to come: lesions on the face, ostracism from society and rejection from friends, ending in hospice care.

An HIV test was still two years away. AIDS was, for all practical purposes, a death sentence. Those who survived were few, inspiring awe, fear and false hope: it could be me, I might have some mutated gene, I'll be the medical mystery they study and write about as they publish their scientific breakthroughs.

"We were talking about your interview," he said, his tone subdued. Whatever lightness we'd enjoyed was dispelled by that cough and my meddling.

"Sure, why not," I replied, equally dispirited. "Forget about the whole romantic fantasy bullshit. It was just a comforting gesture."

He waited.

"Like touching someone's hand who's nervous or who's been crying, just to calm me."

"And why did he need to calm you?"

"Because I found someone I knew dead in a dumpster. It was beyond horrible, Butch."

I started to shiver. Then he, too, reached across and placed his palm over the back of my hand. I hadn't had a chance to tell Butch much about finding Ben in the trash, what it felt like, how frightening it was. Or about the cops coming, or the interview with Mac earlier that day. *Stop calling him Mac,* I said to myself. *He's a stranger. He's a detective. What is wrong with you?*

"It's too much to tell you here, in the middle of one of L.A's most overrated roach traps," I said.

He frowned. "Be nice. We don't have that many lunch options downtown. And besides—"

"It's close to the office," I finished. "That's fine, really. I love seeing you. I just need to talk a lot more than we can in this place."

The waitress came sliding back to the table with a plate in each hand. I wondered if she had wheels on her shoes. At least she didn't have to think about which order went with whom, since we'd asked for the same thing. She put the plates down and left.

"She belongs here," I said.

"We'll go to the taco stand next time. Now eat."

Half his lunch hour was gone. We didn't have any choice but to eat, with quick and general conversation between bites.

"Do me a favor," I said, after taking a third mouthful of sausage and goat cheese wrapped in a skinny pancake.

"I'll call my doctor, don't worry about it."

Worry was all any of us could do when we had no idea what was happening to us, or when we'd move to the head of life's checkout line.

"Now please," he said, "can we talk about something funny? I need to laugh."

Finding anything to laugh about was a bridge too far, but we tried.

Before a hug and a kiss outside, sending Butch in one direction and me back to my car, I told him to stop by the Parrot that night if he was free. I'd be back on shift filling in for Phil. He was expected to be with his mother another day or two and I'd refused to call in reinforcements. I could do this. My new career depended on it. I had found a dead man in a dumpster and survived, just another day in Tinseltown.

"I can't tonight," he said. "I've got a date."

My eyebrows shot up. "Really? *Butch* has a date? I thought you'd given up on that game."

He shrugged, blushing. "Nobody's promised tomorrow, my friend. Might was well take the opportunity if it comes along."

It was a dark way to look at it, but those were dark

times.

"Details," I said.

"Only if it's worth telling you about."

"Fair enough."

I watched Butch walk away and had that too-familiar feeling it was a sight I might not see many more times. That's the way it was in those days. And believe it or not, that's the way it will always be. Butch was right—none of us knows for sure we'll be around tomorrow. Lives can end in seconds, whether it's 1983 in the midst of a plague, or today in a city of millions who won't know you're gone because they never knew you were there.

# TEN

MY SHIFT AT THE PARROT didn't start until six p.m., but I was bored and agitated so I got there early. It had been hard enough killing time after lunch with Butch. From Crepe Stanley's I'd driven home and parked in one of my usual spots on Franklin Avenue, a couple blocks from the apartment. Street parking was the only thing I could afford, since the building I lived in charged an extra $30 a month for a space in the lot. That doesn't seem like much money now, but in 1983 it could make the difference between eating or paying rent.

I seldom drove anywhere. Despite what you hear, lots of people walk in L.A. They take buses, too, and now they take subways that were only a dream back then. *Subways? In L.A.?* The sprawling city wasn't designed for that, and there had been rumors for decades about collusion between General Motors, Standard Oil, and Firestone Tire to destroy the streetcars that once crisscrossed the city. They wanted people dependent on automobiles. Millions of them. But the reality is, you can live in Los Angeles without a car. It just takes planning and determination.

My Gremlin was on its last cylinder. It had served me well for seven years, especially with my escape from Indiana, but the old girl was gasping for breath. Just keeping her running at that point was a significant expense. I was planning to get a better used car as soon as I could save up enough working at the Parrot. It was also another reason I parked on the street—that extra $30 a month could go for a car when I'd stuffed enough tips into my coffee can.

I'd spent a few hours in the apartment watching afternoon television with the sound off. My own thoughts were loud and I couldn't think over the noise of soap operas, game shows or Phil Donahue entertaining an audience of housewives.

At one point I went to my dresser for a clean T-shirt and nearly jumped at what I saw: Ben had left his watch sitting next to my digital clock, the one with the alarm set to start playing KROQ at 10:00 a.m. It was a new wave station in those days. My mornings started with the sounds of The Police, Talking Heads, and Oingo Boingo.

I stared at the watch, a flimsy men's Citizen with a tattered black band. How had I not seen it in the few days since he'd been in my apartment? Why had he left it? Had he been waiting to tell me the next time we spoke, when I was too busy to listen to him? I felt a familiar stab of guilt. Had I not been distracted with work, had I decided Ben was more important than filling some lush's glass of wine, would Ben still be alive?

But there it was, draped atop my pressboard dresser, waiting for Ben. Was that why he'd left it, so he would have to return? It was an old trick, one I'd used myself with men I wanted to see again. Staring at it, I felt accused by it. He was dead now and I was alone at home, looking at the only thing I would ever have of his except the unforgettable sight of his dead eyes.

I picked up the watch and put it in my top dresser drawer. I didn't have to give it to the police. It wasn't evidence. Ben would never need it again. It was mine now.

* * *

Phil was behind the bar when I got to work, surprising me. Josef was still on shift with another hour to go. I only saw him when we traded places—he started at ten and left at six, when Phil and I took over. The other daytimer was Conrad, but he worked weekends and was reported to be attending night school at L.A. City College. That was the basic crew for the parrot, with Derek and Freeze filling in as needed, and our barbacks Brandon, Carlos, and a guy named Dom we suspected was transsexual but weren't sure ('transgender' was not a term in general usage then). Josef was the other long term staff besides Phil, having been there for fifteen years. Everyone else came and went with regularity.

"What are you doing here?" I asked. "I thought you were in Bakersfield with your mom."

"Mom's a drama queen," he said. "The big bad leg break was a sprain. She didn't even need a cast. It was just Mom being needy … and sneaky. It's not the first time she's gotten me to go running home for some emergency that was only in her head."

He finished drying a glass, then said, "Besides, I saw the news about the murder."

"Really? In Bakersfield?"

"Oh yeah, it was a big deal around the whole state. 'Murder at a Hollywood gay bar. No suspects as homosexual community panics.'"

"No one's panicking."

"The media don't care. It's ratings gold. Something's killing us besides AIDS, makes for a nice distraction."

"Well, it got my attention," I said, sliding onto a stool. I waved two fingers at Josef. He filled a glass with ice and bourbon, set it in front of me and walked off down the bar. Bourbon was my drink then—neat, with Coke, or on the rocks, it didn't matter. He set a glass down in front of me and walked away, barely acknowledging me. We tolerated each other, that was about it.

"I'm the one who found the body," I said after taking a sip.

"No shit?" Phil leaned against the cash register, facing me. "What the hell happened?"

"Ben was murdered."

"Ben?"

"He wandered in here last week, looking for LuLu's. New to the city, lost."

"I remember him. Jesus, he was cute. Did you have sex with him?"

I stared at him. "What kind of question is that? Yes, I

did. Then someone strangled him and left him in the dumpster out back."

He could tell he'd crossed a line with me. "I'm sorry. You want to talk about it?"

"Not especially, Phil. I talked about it with the cops last night. I talked about it to a detective this morning. I think I'm all talked out, but thanks for the offer."

I lifted my glass and downed the rest of the bourbon.

"Hey, listen," Phil said, straightening up, "why don't you take the night off?"

"I'm supposed to be filling in for you," I said.

"Well, guess what? I'm here! Go on, Marshall, give yourself a break. Brandon's here to back me up, we'll be fine."

"Really?"

"I insist. You look terrible."

I glanced at myself in the mirror behind the bar. He was right. I looked like someone who hadn't slept for several days. It had only been one night, but maybe the circumstances magnified it. I was tired, I was depressed, and if I stayed at the bar I'd be drunk in an hour.

"Thanks, man," I said. "I'll take you up on that."

I left a dollar on the bar for Josef and headed outside. I wouldn't be able to sleep, not for a few hours at least. I didn't want to go home and stare at my dresser, knowing Ben's watch was in a drawer.

I left the bar and headed to Ivar, another avenue that should be a street. I was familiar with it for the same reason hundreds of other men were. It's where we went for comfort sex—easy, anonymous, fast. I needed some and I knew where to get it.

# ELEVEN

THE HOLLYWOOD SPA LASTED LONGER than most. When it closed in 2014 it was one of the oldest bathhouses in Los Angeles, having handed out its first towels, lube and condoms way back in 1974. I was a horny teenager in an Indiana backwater then, unable to imagine the delights of an open-air sex bazaar. By the time I rolled into Hollywood three years later, the place was in full swing.

For most men, the Spa was where you went to have sex, sometimes lots of it, with people you might never see again. Some you could befriend after an hour or two of delirious bodily-fluid exchange, while others were familiar from previous visits. For a smaller group, the Spa was home. These were the hustlers and the street kids who could scrape up $10 a night for a room and sleep unmolested, if they chose to. Business was seldom conducted at the Spa—prostitution was as illegal then as it is now, and the owners understandably wanted to keep their operating license.

You could always spot the working boys. They hung out in a clique, usually by the pool table. There was a DJ on a platform near the ceiling spinning bass-heavy music intended to make you throb. Throbbing went with the whole motif.

I didn't go as much as I used to those first few years in the city. I wasn't a hustler, aside from a few survival tricks I'd turned when I was new in town. I'd also outgrown anonymous sex, or maybe I'd just had enough of it to satisfy that need for abandon. I was at a time in my life when I hoped that special someone would swagger past on Sunset Boulevard or, as had happened recently, into the Paisley Parrot. He would turn back for a second glance at the same time I did, and we would know it was meant to be.

The thought of Ben made me wince as I slipped my

wallet into one of the long metal boxes they provided for your valuables when you checked in. The entry fee got you a towel and a key on a wrist band that corresponded to either a locker ($6) or a room ($10). I always got a room even if I wasn't planning to spend the night, which I'd only done as a newbie with nowhere else to sleep.

The rooms were narrow, most just wide enough to accommodate a mattress and whoever stepped into the room to check out the goods. Clothes got hung from a hook on the door.

The great thing about a bathhouse is that your objective is obvious and the same as everyone else's. Walking around with a towel wrapped around you dispenses with any need for flirtation or conversation. Unlike a bar, you know exactly what the other guy wants, and, depending on first impressions, you both get it.

The second floor at the Spa was all rooms, with a hallway leading off to a video lounge and another to an intriguing set of stalls for the glory hole fans. My room that night was on the outside, meaning it did not face the stairs and first floor below. I went to the room and quickly undressed. I smelled myself to see if I needed a shower in one of the communal shower rooms; I was fine. I finished stripping, wrapped my towel around my waist and went for a stroll.

A stroll at the Spa meant walking the hallways in a circle, passing the same men over and over. This was especially true when none of them stirred your interest. That happened a lot. It was all timing: if nobody wanted you, or you them, you had to stick around for the new flesh that kept arriving throughout the night or call it quits.

I'd made my second round and was considering leaving when I spotted Freddy. I didn't know his last name, but I knew him as a regular at the Parrot. He was one of the younger customers, clearly a lush but not yet at an age where it showed on his face.

"Hey, Marsh," he said, using a diminutive of my name

I've never liked.

"Hey, Freddy," I replied.

He reached down and brushed his towel. It was involuntary. He wasn't interested in me and I wasn't interested in him, not that way. He preferred men about twenty years older than himself. It takes all kinds, and Freddy would have plenty of opportunities as the night wore on. While the customers may discriminate, the Spa did not. As long as you had the cash and you weren't a troublemaker, you got what you came for most of the time.

I walked past him and finished my circle. Should I go, or stay? It was still very early. I knew I might get lucky if I waited for the after-dinner cruisers. The later it got, the more trade showed up.

I decided to wait it out for another hour or so. I went back to my room, left the door open just in case, and settled onto my narrow mattress, staring at the ceiling with a raised arm under my head.

* * *

I'd never liked the music at the Spa. I didn't like the DJ, either, although we hadn't met and I didn't know his name. You could see him standing in a booth high above the second floor. He always had headphones clipped over his bald head and he rocked back and forth a lot. He thought the rest of us wanted to hear his electronic or house or whatever it was he played, but for some of us it was too subterranean. It relied on overwhelming bass that sometimes made the rooms shake. But as loud as it was, the volume never drowned out the sounds of sex going on around me. Slaps. Grunts. Shouts of ecstasy that occasionally made me wonder if someone should call the police. Nobody had died there, as far as I knew, but it would not surprise me to find out a few went missing.

I glanced at my watch on the small ledge where I'd laid it next to a pack of cigarettes. You could smoke at the baths and it helped pass the time. When I saw a second hour had gone by, I swung my feet around and sat up, staring for a moment at the floor. It was time to admit defeat and go home.

"Well, what a surprise," a familiar voice said. "Or maybe not?"

I looked up and instantly blushed a deep red. Standing in my doorway, his arm stretched up along the doorframe and a towel that looked about to drop, stood Detective Kevin McElroy. *Mac*. The man who earlier that day had questioned me about Ben's murder. *The man whose hand had touched mine in a way I no longer thought was accidental.*

"Mac?" I asked. I knew it was him, but the one-word question implied much more than it said, like, *Why are you at the baths? Do homicide detectives often come here? Or is this some kind of undercover operation and you're looking for suspects?*

"I'm glad we're past 'Detective McElroy'," he said, smiling. It was the smile that did it, goddamn him. Imperfect white teeth, lips that could have been airbrushed, they were so … *right*.

"What are you doing here?" I said.

"I thought this was a bathhouse."

"Well, yeah, it is … but you're a cop."

"You think cops don't have sex?"

I shrugged, not knowing how to respond.

He turned and looked down the hallway, glancing left, then right. "Say, listen, can I come in? I'm not really the doorway type."

I was helpless. It was a small room, and there he was, so close to me I could reach out and touch him, which is exactly what I did.

For the next two hours we explored each other's bodies, savoring, exhausting, starting over. And then, amazingly, we slept.

# TWELVE

I HADN'T SPENT AN ENTIRE night at the baths since I'd first arrived in Hollywood and had nowhere else to go. Maybe that's why I always left before I could fall asleep—waking up on a mattress in what amounted to an indoor sex market brought back memories I wanted kept away. I was a successful bartender now, with an apartment I paid for myself, bills that were never past due, and a checking account without a single overdraft since my first deposit. Once a hustler, *not always* a hustler, and when the afterglow of furious sex wore off I was ready to get out of there.

I had no idea what time it was when I woke up. There are no windows in a bathhouse, and few clocks. I sleep on my side, and when my eyes opened I instinctively reached for my watch: 6:00 a.m. Jesus, I'd slept for six hours. Had I been that comfortable with Mac? I rolled over to see if he was awake, too, and found no one on the bed beside me. He'd left me there sometime after I'd drifted off to sleep. Had he gone immediately? Or had he lingered an hour or so replaying our sex in his mind?

*You're just another trick to him, Marshall,* I thought. *Warm flesh in a sea of it. And a fool.* It's easy, when a man has his fingers entwined in yours and his gaze fixed on you, to think it might be something more. The fantasy doesn't happen every time, but enough to make you feel like you've been had by your own ridiculous longing. Cupid shot his arrow into you, then twisted the barbed arrowhead and yanked it back out. Love is something we fall into and out of as easily as daydreams.

In my case it had been a night dream. A wet, hot, sticky, hours-long night dream. He was a cop. I was a bartender. He was thirty-six, I was twenty-five. *What the hell was wrong with me?* Butch once told me that expectations are disappointments waiting to happen. He was right.

Crying has never been my thing, so I did not shed a tear for the death of my fantasy. Instead I quickly dressed, wanting to get home to my own shower and my toothbrush—the pleasant taste of last night in my mouth had been overwhelmed by morning breath.

I finished tucking in my shirt and putting on my socks and shoes. I reached for my coat on the back of the door—January mornings are cold in Los Angeles. As I reached for the coat I felt something in my shirt pocket. Odd. I slipped my fingers into the pocket and found another business card. It was the second time he'd given it to me. Maybe he thought I'd thrown the first one away and wanted to make his point.

Detective Kevin McElroy had left me a message.

* * *

The French Market lasted about as long as the Hollywood Spa. Opened in 1973, the restaurant and small shopping complex closed in 2015 with much lamenting from the surrounding West Hollywood community, especially its older residents. There's something melancholic about long lasting gay establishments going out of business after forty years or more. It can remind us of ourselves, the men and women who enjoyed the thrill of these places in our youth, the excitement of being around so many people like us. They're part of our history, collectively and individually, and their passing brings back memories of times when being gay still meant you needed shelter, you needed bars and bathhouses and restaurants where you felt accepted and unthreatened.

The restaurant inside the French Market, called the French Quarter, was still very much alive the morning I left the Spa with Mac's card in my hand. It was no longer in my shirt pocket because I'd been so excited by the message he wrote that I kept it cupped in my palm. The words were simple and explicit: *Let's do this again*, followed by the same home phone number he'd given me before.

It doesn't take much for any of us to experience the thrill of a possible relationship. A glance held beyond passing, a hand on an arm, a "What are you doing Tuesday night?" In this case, Mac and I had feasted on each other for several hours. Now I had his card in my hand and his home phone number, *underlined*. The only question was how long I'd wait before calling.

The French Quarter had an outside seating area but it was still too chilly for me to sit and watch the traffic on Santa Monica Boulevard. I got a table inside, across from a shop called Dorothy's Surrender that sold greeting cards, key chains, gag items and lots of rainbow tchotchkes.

On the way in I'd picked up a copy of that day's Los Angeles Times. I enjoyed reading the paper with a cup of coffee. The waiter filled my cup, took my order for eggs, toast, bacon and pancakes, and sped away. I'd burned off a couple thousand calories with Mac, and I was hungry.

I'd barely taken my first sip of hot coffee when I nearly spit it out. On the first page of the paper, below the fold, was an item with the headline, *"Murder at Second Gay Club."* Short and indifferent, it read:

*Police discovered the dismembered body of a man stuffed in several garbage bags behind Hollywood's notorious Red River homosexual nightclub.*

The Red River was a bar, not a nightclub, a distinction without a difference to a hack reporter covering dead gay men. It was also the Paisley Parrot's shabby twin, often the second stop on a drunk's nightly descent into oblivion. I continued reading.

*This is the second brutal murder in two days, leading authorities to speculate they were committed by the same person. The first victim has been identified as Bentley Wennig, twenty-*

*seven years old, originally from Bellevue, Washington. His body was found early Monday morning in a dumpster behind the Paisley Parrot, another club known to be frequented by homosexuals. Police have not yet released the identity of the second victim, pending notification of the victim's family.*

That's all it said. I wondered why the writer had referred to the Red River as 'notorious.' Maybe he had a dim view of gay people, or maybe he just wanted to sneak in a little tabloid spice. I thought it was unbecoming of a paper as reputable as the *Times*.

After having an angry conversation with the reporter in my head, I wondered who the dead man was. Did I know him? Was he a customer of the Parrot's as well? We shared many of the same patrons, stumbling the three blocks between bars as they blotted out consciousness. How many parts had he been cut into? How many bags had been left in the alley with his limbs inside? I knew the nighttime bartender there, a guy named Toby. We'd spent a forgettable hour in his bed once, several years earlier. I'd call us acquaintances, but we knew each other well enough for me to make a stop there on the way to work that night. If he wasn't on duty, I'd just talk up whoever was working and get some information from them, starting with the dead man's name if he knew it.

My hands were trembling. I set the paper down and looked around me. There were happy, smiling people, many of them my gay brethren, enjoying another breakfast on another morning in West Hollywood. Was someone coming for us? Would the smell of panic soon waft through the air like cigarette smoke?

I didn't know. They didn't know. I doubted even Mac knew at that point. I took his card out of my pocket as the waiter arrived with my food. I wasn't hungry anymore but I would at least eat the eggs. Then I would head home and make a phone call.

# THIRTEEN

I WALKED HOME FROM THE French Quarter in a daze. My thoughts were a jumble after reading the article. Two murders in two nights. Bodies left at separate but similar gay bars. As I walked along Hollywood Boulevard to Highland I had the unsettling idea the killer had intended for his victims to be found, not quite on display, but not hidden where they might decompose for days or weeks before someone stumbled upon a half-rotten corpse. Did that mean the victims weren't random? The notion that they had been targeted because of something they had in common was farfetched. And what would that be, anyway? *That they drank at the same bar*? We all drank at the same bars, that's how we knew each other. Besides, Ben had only been in town for a few days. What could he possibly have in common with Freddy?

I was making myself crazy with speculation. The one person I hoped could enlighten me had left his card in my shirt pocket after a night of sex at the baths. I took it out again and stared at is as I turned up Highland toward my apartment.

Kevin McElroy. *Mac.* Detective First Grade, whatever that meant, Hollywood Division. The phone number listed was probably to the station, it didn't look like a direct line. The other number, the one he'd given me twice now, was his home phone with an 818 area code. I had no idea what hours he worked, except that he'd been on duty at three in the morning when I'd found Ben's body. For all I knew he slept during the day. I would if I had the graveyard shift—a name that sounded appropriate at that moment. I decided to take a chance and call him at home. At worst I'd get his voicemail and leave a message. He may not even know yet about the second murder. Did I want to be the one to tell him?

Or, to be honest, did I simply want to hear his voice again? It contained just a bit of gravel, a touch of roughness that, when speaking against my ear, had left me shivering.

*A man's dead,* I told myself as I took my keys out, walking up to my apartment building. *You might want to think about something besides Mac for just a minute.*

It wouldn't be easy calling him, but waiting could be fatal for another innocent victim. I knew something dark and threatening had stepped onto the small stage of our lives and demanded our attention.

I got into my apartment and saw it was ten o'clock. I'd managed to kill a few hours walking and having breakfast, but it still seemed early to call Mac. I made a pot of coffee, knowing I would not be sleeping any time soon, and sat at my kitchen table for another hour staring at the minute hand on the kitchen clock. It finally struck eleven and I went into the living room. I sat on my green-and-yellow plaid couch, the one I'd picked up at a thrift store, and reached for the phone.

## FOURTEEN

I EXPECTED TO GET AN answering machine. I assumed Mac slept during the day after working the overnight shift. I also wanted to think I'd tired him out with the strenuous sex we'd had at the Spa on a mattress made for one. I guessed he didn't rise before noon. I knew something about this kind of schedule: the Parrot closed at two a.m., often later with stragglers and having to escort two or three drunken ones out the door.

I'd prepared my speech, keeping it to sixty seconds. Just when I'd taken a breath and was about to start my, 'Hi, Mac, this is Marshall ...' soliloquy, the phone picked up.

"Mac here," he said.

Two words, no preface.

"Mac?" I asked, as if he hadn't been clear enough.

"Marshall?"

*Oh, good,* I thought. *He recognizes my voice. Maybe this is going somewhere.*

I wasn't expecting it. Taken off guard, I said, "Uh ... yeah, it's me, Marshall. Why are you up so early?"

Stupid question number one.

"You called to ask me why I'm up so early?" he said. There wasn't a trace of fatigue in his voice, no remnant of sleep.

I feared losing him if I could not make a convincing case for calling so soon and unprepared.

"I was wondering if you'd read the news. Or seen it on TV, or something ..."

"*What* news? What are you talking about?"

One thing I always liked about Mac, and have always remembered, was his way of getting to the point. He wasn't bothered by a phone call this early, or a call from someone he'd only spoken to in a murder investigation and a darkened bathhouse. He just wanted me to be direct.

"There's been a second murder," I said. "It was in the L.A. Times."

Pause. "What? *When*?"

*Last night when you were pressed against me*, I thought.

"Sometime in the middle of the night, just like Ben Wennig at the Parrot."

"I know where Wennig was found."

Did I detect irritation in his voice? Did he dislike being told what he already knew? Note to self …

"I wasn't on shift last night," he said, stating the obvious since he'd been with me and didn't know about the second killing. "One of the other detectives would have taken the call." Stopping to think, he said, "Bastardo."

*Did he just call me a bastard?* "Excuse me?"

"Lou Bastardo, he's the lead when I'm off. I'm just surprised he didn't page me."

People had pagers in those pre-cell phone days: cops, doctors, hustlers and drug dealers.

Another moment passed. "Ah, crap," he said, and I guessed he had looked at his pager. "It's there. I must have slept through it."

"So you do sleep. I wasn't sure."

"Four hours a night, usually. "

I did a quick calculation in my head. If he slept four hours, and he'd slept through the page, and he'd left me asleep at the baths, the body must have been found ...

"Sunrise," he said, finishing my thought. "I crashed from four to eight. Not my usual time for that, but I was tuckered out."

I could hear his smile, a slight bending in the air. And I was beyond charmed that he'd said 'tuckered.' It made me think of all the places that *weren't* Los Angeles, the towns and small communities where people talked like that. I wondered where he came from—it was among the hundred things we'd not taken time to discuss while we were busy exploring each other's bodies.

"What did the article say?" he asked.

"Very few details," I replied. "The reporter used the words 'notorious' and 'homosexual,' and he gave Ben's name as a murder victim found the night before. But not much else."

"Because they don't know anything."

"Obviously."

"The media, I mean," he said. "That doesn't mean LAPD doesn't have information. I wasn't there, I didn't even know about it until just now. But you can't assume anything based on a sketchy news report."

He waited a long moment, then said, "I'm glad you called, by the way. It means you got my card."

"Twice. This one you left it in my shirt pocket, it was hard to miss."

"Yeah, well, I was hoping you'd call, just not under these circumstances. Listen, Marshall, I need to contact the station."

"Are you in trouble for missing the page?"

"Don't worry about it. And no, it's not that unusual. If it was urgent he would have called. The page was a courtesy. I'll just tell him I was in the shower and then fell asleep. He's the same grade as I am, it's his case unless ..."

I waited. Anticipation has never been pleasant for me.

"Unless *what*?" I finally prompted.

"Unless the murders are linked."

Linked. As in related. As in someone is killing gay men and leaving their corpses behind bars.

"You mean the same killer."

"Not necessarily. There could be some other reason the victims are connected besides who killed them. Listen, I can't get into this and I really need to go."

"I understand. I just wanted to see if you'd heard about it."

"When will I see you again?"

No pussyfooting around. That was Mac.

"Your wish is my command," I said.

"Ah, stop that right now, you'll distract me."

"Is that a bad thing?"

"When I have to go to work, yes. I'll call you, okay?"

Somehow I knew this was not a brush off.

"I'll be here."

"You have a pager?"

I really wanted to say yes. Instead I said, "It's on order, I'm picking it up today. I'll get the number to you."

"Great," he said. I was sure he knew I was improvising. "Got a pencil? Take my pager number down, then just beep me with yours."

Keeping the phone cradled between my cheek and shoulder, I hurried to the bookshelf for a pen and paper. Luckily the phone cord was long enough to reach without ripping it out of the wall.

"Go ahead," I said.

That was the beginning of something wonderful, amazing, excruciating, terrifying, and life changing. But at the moment all I knew was that Mac McElroy, homicide investigator, rising star in the movie of my life, was giving me a pager number I remember to this day.

And I always will.

# FIFTEEN

A DAY THAT WOULD NORMALLY be free until I went to work was now jam-packed. I'd lied to Mac about getting a pager, conveniently on the day he asked me if I owned one. I had to remedy that quickly. I wanted us to be able to reach each other at a moment's notice. It's hard to imagine a world where phones were not miniature handheld computers, plug-ins to the internet and social media. Once upon a time, people used pay phones if they needed to reach someone during their daily travels. It's a baffling concept to kids today, and a fading memory for the rest of us.

There were several stores along Hollywood Boulevard that sold pagers. They were popular then—a status symbol for those who needed them and many others who pretended to. Some people even wore pagers that didn't work, just to keep up appearances.

Hollywood Boulevard in the 1980s was less a boulevard of broken dreams than a seedy stretch of souvenir shops, sex toy retailers, and movie theaters with sticky floors. The world famous Frederick's of Hollywood was a major draw, along with the Hollywood Wax Museum. Frederick's sold sex, the wax museum sold glamour, both of them specialized in illusion.

When I walked into Manny's Electronics I was surprised to see someone I knew working behind the counter. I'd known Dennis as a street kid when I'd first moved to L.A. He wasn't a kid anymore, and it was good to see him working a straight job.

"Marshall?" he said, looking up from a newspaper. There was no one else in the store and I thought for a moment the place might be a front for money laundering. It wasn't unheard of.

"Dennis?"

"Damn, you look good."

"You, too. I'm surprised ..."

"To see me alive?" he said, smiling. I could see he had not spent any of his hard-earned pay on better teeth.

"I didn't say that."

"But you thought it. That's okay. I figured you'd be dead by now, too, or gone back to wherever you came from."

"Indiana."

"Right. They call them hosers or something."

"Hoosiers."

"Same thing. So what are you looking for?"

"I need a good pager."

His eyebrows shot up. "You hustling again? You're getting a little old for that."

I suddenly remembered not liking Dennis all that much. "It's not for that, or for drugs. I have a boyfriend and we need to be able to reach each other."

*A boyfriend? Are you out of your mind?* I thought. *You had sex at the baths. He might consider you a suspect in a murder, and suddenly he's your boyfriend? Get a grip, Marshall.*

I shook off my doubts and told Dennis I was in a hurry. With little additional small talk, he steered me to a cheap and reliable pager and I was on my way, content with the thought that if I never saw Dennis again it would be fine with me.

* * *

The Red River had been around longer than the Paisley Parrot by three or four years. Both old hags showed their age, and both served the same clientele.

The River, as we called it, was tucked away on De Longpre Avenue, near Seward. Like the Parrot, it had kept a low profile for so long it was nearly invisible to anyone who wasn't looking for it. And, like the Parrot, it was mob-owned. Same mob, same scam. The current owners of record were fronts for the mafia, needed for their names on the lease and license, but otherwise of use only to keep the place running. This had been true through a succession of bars beginning in the 1950s. Homosexuality was a crime when the bars first opened, and criminals needed places to gather where they could enjoy themselves without too much fear of police raids that were kept to a minimum with a weekly envelope of cash into the right hands. Payoffs and graft went with the job description—when you worked for the mob, you played by mob rules, or you left town one way or another. The two bars even had the same overseer: Fat Dick. He was as familiar to the bar staff as he was dreaded. Where Dick went, intimidation followed. We were always happy to see him leave with his weekly skim.

I got there at two p.m. knowing the place would not be empty. Alcoholics don't pay attention to the time of day, and the lucky ones—the ones on disability, the ones living off scams, or the odd rich ones—could drink around the clock, stopping only to pass out for a few hours each night when the bars shut down.

"Hey," I said to Garland when I walked in. He was the daytime bartender at the River. I knew him from around, the way I knew a lot of people, and I sometimes stopped in for a burger and fries. The River sold food, unlike the Parrot. It wasn't half bad, if you didn't mind your lunch with a mouthful of second hand cigarette smoke and the smell of Lysol from a mopped floor.

"What's up, Marshall?" he said.

We'd never hooked up and I'd never wanted to. I'd heard things about Garland's tastes in bondage and forms of pain.

I took a seat at the bar. "Not much," I said, "if you consider body parts run of the mill."

"You heard," he said, sliding a bourbon and Coke in front of me. It was early, but accepting a drink on the house was always a good move. People get offended at the silliest things.

"Everybody heard. It was in the paper. Poor Rudy.

Must've been him who found the body, right? He in yet?"

"Yeah, it was him. He doesn't come in till four, and after last night he may not come back. I'll know when he shows up, or doesn't."

"Wow," I said, taking a quick sip. "You know it's the second murder in two nights."

He'd been leaning against the bar watching me. He always did this when I came in. Just because we hadn't had sex didn't mean he wasn't interested. He stood up straight, pushing back with his hands.

"Two murders, seriously? I wasn't aware of that. It's not like nobody ever gets killed in Hollywood. I knew Rudy found the guy last night … parts of him, whatever, but not about another one."

"Oh yeah, it's a big deal. One body at the Parrot, one here. I found the first victim," I said, suddenly ashamed at the way I'd said it, as if I were proud of it.

"Go on!"

"Really, I did. A guy who'd just come to town and who I'd … I was hoping to get to know."

"Well, it's a good thing you didn't."

"How so?"

"It could have been you! You could have been in the wrong place at the wrong time with this man. You could both be dead."

It was ridiculous speculation. I took another long sip of my drink, letting the familiar warmth rush over me. My fondness for intoxication had always been there, but I'd been keeping it at bay."

"The cops were back this morning," Garland said. "They asked me if I remembered any shady customers in here yesterday. I had to keep from laughing. Most of the people who drink here are shady."

He leaned closer, lowering his voice. "I'll tell you what, I'm more worried about Fat Dick and the Bianchis than I am about some freak killing his tricks."

I winced at that. I doubted Ben had been a killer's trick.

At the very least, I *wanted* to doubt it. But maybe he'd taken our short conversation that night as a blow-off. Maybe he thought I wasn't interested so he went cruising and got himself killed.

"What's Fat Dick got to do with it?" I asked.

"Are you kidding me? Think about it, Marshall. They've got a good thing going here, and at the Parrot. They've got cash cows that give them bags of money every week. They've got whatever else kind of criminal shit they're running out of these bars, and along comes a serial killer. You think business is going to pick up? Body bags are bad for the bottom line, my friend."

He was right, but there was nothing Fat Dick or the entire Bianchi clan could do about a psychopath, except get to him before the cops did. That seemed an unlikely scenario to me.

I finished my drink. He motioned at the glass; I shook my head no, one was enough.

"You think there's a connection between the two murders?" he asked.

"It seems possible."

"What, like a serial killer?"

"Shhh!" I said, glancing at the other three customers sitting at the bar.

"Oh please, they're too interested in their booze to care what we're talking about."

He was right. My fellow patrons were nursing their third or fourth drinks and staring at a TV mounted on the back wall.

"I'm not saying it was a serial killer," I said. "Maybe two bodies dumped at two gay bars in two nights is a coincidence. But something's going on."

"Could be loan sharks."

"I don't think so. Cutting someone's arms and legs off is extreme, even for the mob."

"Some other vendetta, then. Who knows how a killer's mind works."

"Did you know him?" I asked.

"The killer?"

"No, stupid! The victim. The guy Rudy found chopped up and packaged in the trash."

"Rudy didn't get a good look at the head, if that's what you mean," he said. "He was too busy puking, from what I heard. And if the cops know who it was they're not saying. Maybe they don't have an ID yet. Maybe whoever did it kept the guy's wallet, or he didn't carry one to begin with. Half the drunks in here don't bring their wallets. The tabs I keep, let me tell you."

I'd learned next to nothing in twenty minutes. I don't know what I'd expected. The inside scoop? To what? Garland clearly had no information.

It was still too early for my shift at the Parrot but I had nothing else to do. I didn't want to go home where I would just stare at the phone or my new pager hoping Mac would summon me. Home was the most boring place I could think of being, so I thanked Garland, slipped a tip on the counter and headed out. Phil might be on duty by now, or just hanging out again—he practically lived at the Parrot. His company, along with whoever was drinking their way to a blackout by now, was better than none.

## SIXTEEN

SENSATION SELLS, AND NOTHING MAKES better copy than a murder story—in this case two of them. I saw the front page story in the Blaze as soon as I opened the Parrot's door. The Blaze was a throwaway paper, the kind you found stacked outside gay bars, restaurants and bathhouses. Half of it was stories of interest to the gay community. Another quarter was advertising, and the rest was personal ads. In the pre-internet, pre-sex app days, men used small personal ads in the gay rags as a way to find each other when they weren't cruising the usual hangouts.

I grabbed the paper and headed for a barstool. Sure enough, Phil was already there washing glasses in the sink under the counter. I was surprised to see Derek on duty, dropping off a vodka rocks to a some old crow at the end of the bar fumbling with a pack of cigarettes while he hacked up a wad of pre-cancerous phlegm.

"Where's Josef?" I asked, sliding into place. Josef should have been working.

Phil looked up at me. Tapping his nose to indicate too much sniffing of cocaine, he said, "Called in with the 'flu.'"

"Again?"

"He's susceptible to it. What are you doing here so early?"

"Restless," I said. "There was another murder."

Phil put the glass away and looked at me. "Here?"

"No! I think you'd know if there was another murder at the Parrot. This was over at the Red River."

"Jesus Christ. Seriously?"

I slapped the paper down on the bar and punched it several times with my fingers. "It's already in the papers, including the Blaze."

He came close and leaned over, looking at the front

page. I turned it sideways so we could both read it.

*Popper Jack Strikes Again! Second Gay Man Murdered*

I hadn't read the headline carefully when I snatched up the paper. I'd seen the 'Second Gay May Murdered' line, but not the 'Popper Jack.'

"What the hell?" I said, as we kept reading.

*Police are moving fast on a case that could spread panic in the gayborhood. Two men in two nights, each found horribly murdered, each outside a well-known gay bar. Is a killer on the prowl?*

The article, written by someone named Brad Herring, went on to briefly describe what was known about the killings: victim one, Bentley Wennig, had been found in a dumpster behind the Paisley Parrot. I knew about that one, I'd found him. The second night they discovered victim two dismembered and left in trash bags behind the Red River. Then, to my complete shock, the article identified the second man as Freddy Carpenter.

"Oh my God," I said, staring at the newsprint.

"What is it?"

"Freddy … I never knew his last name, but I saw him at the baths. It must have been just a couple hours before he was killed."

"Freddy? *Our* Freddy? Vodka martini straight up, pearl olives?"

"That's the guy."

Phil knew most customers by their drinks. We all did.

"Wow," he said. Then he stepped back as if I'd coughed in his face. "You're bad luck, dude, seriously. Maybe you should take some time off, go to another continent."

He was trying to be funny in a very serious situation.

"Fuck off," I said. "What I want to know is how this reporter knew it was Freddy. And why he called the killer

'Popper Jack.'"

The answer was in the next paragraph.

*Sources inside the police department said both victims were found with full, unopened bottles of amyl nitrite, also known as 'poppers', in their shirt pockets. Speculation within the homicide division is that the killer left them as a calling card.*

Cute, I thought. We can't even report on something as gruesome and terrifying as a serial killer without giving him a catchy nickname. *Son of Sam, the Boston Strangler, the Stiletto Rapist*. And now, with its distinctly gay twist, *Popper Jack*.

I knew what poppers were, having pressed an opened bottle beneath my nostrils a time or two. The high produces a sudden lightheadedness that heightens and intensifies a sexual experience, as least for the minute or so the effect lasts.

The article didn't say much more. As informed as the reporter appeared to be, he either didn't have more details or he wasn't revealing them.

"How would the writer know these things?" I asked.

"Maybe he's screwing someone in the police department."

I blushed. Phil didn't know about me and Mac but my immediate response was guilt, as if I was somehow part of all this by sleeping with a cop.

"Or maybe he just has a source who enjoys seeing their leaks in print," I said.

I was sure Mac would not want this kind of information given out before the police were ready to release it. I also guessed he wouldn't like some reporter from a gay newspaper tagging a serial killer with a name they'd now be stuck with.

"How's your mother?" I asked, sliding the paper away. I'd had enough of murders and victims for the moment.

"My mother?" he said, perplexed.

"She sprained her ankle, remember?"

"Oh, right!" he said, and I was struck by the strangeness of it. How could he forget having taken off for Bakersfield to help a mother in distress?

"She's fine, walking with crutches for a few days. Considering she doesn't do anything but drink, smoke and chase kids out of her yard, I think she'll be okay. There was no reason for me to stay—not with what's going on here." He nodded at the paper. "Should I get a gun for protection?"

"Oh for godsake, no. Do you even know what to do with one?"

"Aim, pull the trigger, watch out for blood splatter."

"You're a funny man, Phil," I said. "Except when you try to be. Could I please get a drink?"

"Before your shift? You must be upset."

That was an understatement. In the course of forty-eight hours I'd found one man I'd slept with dead in a dumpster, and another I'd seen at the baths was left in pieces behind the Red River bar. On top of it all I was falling in serious like with a homicide detective who might like me back, or who might be playing me while he waited to put me in handcuffs.

"Just the drink, please. I'll let it wear off before I start."

"Good," he said. "I'm glad we're together tonight. This is getting scary. And I don't just mean that psycho who's killing people."

"What are you talking about?"

"The Bianchis."

I stared at him. Murder was bad for business, that was obvious, but why would the Bianchis care about a few dead customers? It wasn't like there weren't plenty more to take their place.

Phil lowered his voice and leaned toward me. "All I know is that Fat Dick is worried."

I started to ask Phil how he knew this, then thought better of it. Phil was a man of few scruples and I'd heard he wasn't above having sex with Fat Dick now and then for some extra cash.

"The Bianchis can't blame us for a serial killer," I said.

"These are Fat Dick's bars. The Bianchis run them behind the scenes, but Fat Dick is the boss. They don't want the publicity this is bringing and they told Dick in so many words to do something about it."

"That's crazy," I said. "He can't do anything about it."

The ownership of the Parrot and the Red River was a maze of names, entities and licenses that would take an expert mapmaker to unravel. The Paisley Parrot was ostensibly owned by someone named Oscar LeGrand. But as far as any of us knew, there was no Oscar LeGrand. While I had no doubt he'd once been a living, breathing person, it could be that the Bianchis extracted whatever they needed from him, then dropped him into a cement foundation somewhere or off a boat where his body would be eaten before it could float onto the beach. Fat Dick was the only manager we knew.

"Well," said Phil, wiping the counter with a damp rag, "he's freaked out, and a freaked out Fat Dick is a dangerous Fat Dick.

He was right. Between a killer stalking us and Fat Dick wanting to make sure he wasn't blamed by the Bianchis for any slowdown in their cash flow, things were looking bleak. I wasn't sure working together that night would make us feel any safer, but I needed to be around someone and Phil was a familiar presence. I couldn't call Mac, not yet. I couldn't sound worried, and I wasn't ready to say I'd seen Freddy at the baths. It was bad enough being connected to one murder. Two could be more trouble than I'd bargained for.

# SEVENTEEN

I WOKE UP WITH A massive hangover sometime around 9:00 a.m. That was an unusual occurrence for me then—I didn't find myself in a state of perpetual hangover until my 30s—and a distinctly unpleasant one. It took a lot to give me a hangover, usually enough drinks to induce a brownout, the sort of in-and-out-of-it haze where I would remember parts of conversations and flashes of behavior accompanied with the dreaded questions, 'Did I really do that? Did I really say that?'

To make matters worse, I'd gotten plastered at work. This wasn't strictly prohibited, but it was frowned upon. The guys who operated bars on behalf of the mob were a small consortium of aging gay men serving at the Bianchis' pleasure. The only one I ever met was named Claude, a wispy old thing in his 70s who was an owner of the Red River along with another man who may or may not have existed. Men in Claude's line of work were once called 'aunties', gay men who owned and operated bars for the mafia. Sometimes it was just one man, sometimes it was a corporation formed for the sole purpose of creating businesses that laundered very dirty money.

I wasn't going to get fired. Oscar LeGrand was not coming back to life to send me packing. Fat Dick wasn't due in until Wednesday to take the Bianchis' cut. Phil had been there last night to pick up the slack and keep me from making any major mistakes, and frankly I functioned pretty well in those days with eight drinks in me. I didn't make a fool of myself. I didn't start any conflicts with customers I disliked. I didn't hit on anyone. I just drank too much, on the job. I made it through my shift, took Phil's advice that I leave early around 1:00 a.m., and went home to pass out.

Now I was suffering the consequences. I can testify from

experience that chemotherapy is worse that the worst hangover you could ever have, but not by much. My head felt like a melon someone had smashed with a hammer. My mouth tasted like dog shit smothered in tree bark. I'm sure it smelled as bad, too. My vision was blurred and I had to keep squinting up at the ceiling to focus.

"Ah, shit," I said to the empty apartment. I'd felt the wetness on the sheets and realized I had pissed myself.

I managed to crawl out of bed. After putting on a dry pair of briefs, I made a pot of coffee. I needed something to get me going, to propel me into the new day and out of the old night.

* * *

Two hours later I was feeling better. While it wasn't by much, it was desperately needed. The more distance I could put between myself and the previous night's events, the better. *Nothing happened,* I told myself. *You drank too much, it was probably obvious, but hell, they were all drunker than you.* Knowing that almost everyone at the Parrot drank more than I did helped me stave off creeping self-pity.

I'd flipped the mattress and changed the sheets. I'd endured a shower and taken out the trash. I was feeling just about human again when I turned on the twelve o'clock news and watched it lead with "Two gruesome murders in two days … what we know now."

'We' was a woman reporter standing in front of the Red River with a microphone, big blond hair, unnaturally white teeth and an unusual amount of exposed cleavage for someone with a career in TV journalism. She'd look good on a stripper pole and knew it.

I listened as she repeated what had been in the Blaze story, with some added personal information about Freddy Carpenter. My mouth dropped open when I heard the words "wife and two young children." Freddy? *A wife and kids*? But he was just another lush spending his nights on a stool in a gay bar. How could someone like that keep either of his lives a secret—the one he showed us at the Parrot, and the one he showed his family at home? I'd slept with a few married men since coming out in high school (in a small Indiana town you usually found yourself cruised by a guy with a wedding ring), but I hadn't known anyone with such a stark contrast between who we thought he was and who he *really* was.

There was a short video clip of the same reporter knocking on the front door of a house. I couldn't peg the neighborhood, but it looked like most of them in Southern California—stucco, clay tiled roof, beige in every way. It could be Los Feliz, or the Wilshire District, or whatever straight section of West Hollywood existed at the time. No one answered the door and it cut back to Blondie talking to camera outside the bar.

"We've still had no comment from the victim's wife or family, except to ask for privacy during this difficult time."

*Yeah, well, pounding on the door of a widow who just found out her husband was a homo was not very respectful of her privacy.*

I grabbed the remote and turned off the TV. I was slowly recovering from the worst hangover in memory and I didn't need lurid details clanging around in my brain.

I'd just set the remote back on the coffee table when the phone rang. It made me jump. It was one of those post-princess phones that were common then, avocado green, a skinny loaf of plastic shouting at me.

My hand shot out and grabbed the phone off the end table. Holding it in one hand, I picked up the receiver with the other.

"Hello?"

"Hey."

It was that voice. *Mac's* voice. So deep and hot it sounded like phone sex when you were talking about the weather.

"Oh … hey," I said, hoping he couldn't hear the effects

of last night's bad behavior in my voice.

"What's going on? How are you? I called the bar last night."

*Uh-oh.* "Sorry I couldn't talk," I said.

There was a pause. "But we did talk."

"Yeah, of course, I just meant …"

"You were wasted, Marshall, really fucked up. But it's okay, I'm not your mother. I'm not going to judge you, and I won't run away …"

*You won't run away from me? Maybe you should get a second opinion.*

"… But drinking on the job is a really bad idea. And drinking that much anytime is a worse one."

"Tell me about it," I said. "Fortunately the only boss there was Phil and I've covered his ass a time or two. This never happens, by the way."

It was a true statement when I said it. The binge drinking didn't start for several more years.

"What did we talk about?" I steeled myself. Being told what you'd said when you were drunk is one of life's most unpleasant experiences.

I could hear a smile in his voice, if such a thing is possible. "You told me how much you wanted to kiss me."

*And*?

"And how fast you were falling for me."

*Boom.*

"Listen, Mac, I wasn't in my right mind …"

"So it's not true?"

"I didn't say that. I just mean it's not something I *would* say this early in … whatever this is."

"It's a murder investigation."

It stopped me cold. He was right. There were victims to consider, a killer, grieving loved ones. Here I was thinking it was all about finding my soul mate.

"Hey, I was kidding," he said. My silence must have given me away. "Bad time for a joke that doesn't sound like one. I'm sorry."

"You're right, you know. It's a murder investigation, and I'm a witness, if not a suspect."

He didn't answer that.

"How about lunch?" he said.

I still felt woozy and my stomach lurched at the thought of food, but I wasn't going to tell him that.

"Say where and I'll meet you."

"My place."

Now I was truly baffled. Was he toying with me? Did he think I'd confess with our clothes off? And why his place?

"Sure," I said, not wanting to hesitate too long.

"Got a pen?"

"I'll remember the address."

"Good enough. If you don't, you've got my phone number."

"And your pager. If I didn't know better I'd think you wanted me around."

"You're as smart as I thought you were, Marshall James."

He proceeded to give me an address in Glendale. I could be there in a half hour.

We hung up with "See you soon." I headed into the bathroom for a quick second shower, just to be sure. The more hot water I ran over myself, the more last night's drunkenness and the morning's regret faded away.

# EIGHTEEN

LOS ANGELES IS A HODGEPODGE of neighborhoods and vicinities; you can pass from one into another with no indication you've gone from Los Feliz to Hollywood, or Hollywood to Beachwood Canyon, or even into the separate city of Glendale. Every place melts into the next, providing L.A. with its famous sense of sprawl.

I left my apartment around 12:30 p.m., drove east on Franklin Avenue, then along Los Feliz Boulevard past the Greek Theatre, Griffith Park, and eventually into the city of Glendale. It always felt like an enclave to me, a bubble of white homogeny where the rents were a little cheaper and the lifestyle more manicured. By 1:00 p.m. I was parked in front of a generic stucco two-story apartment building with the name *Orchid Estates* in chipped italics on the front wall. There has always been a bit of overstatement to Southern California. Apartment complexes of no special note call themselves 'estates' and unimpressive streets call themselves avenues. It's as if the city began with an inferiority complex it never overcame.

Parking, however, was abundant. I never had trouble finding a spot, unlike Manhattan where you're lucky to get something after twenty minutes circling the block.

It was easy enough to find Mac's apartment—his name was on the panel of buzzers: *McElroy, 2J.* I pressed it and two seconds later the door gave off that shrill, abrasive buzz of front doors everywhere. There was a second glass door inside it that sounded as soon as the first one closed behind me.

To my surprise, there was a courtyard inside with a pool. They're not uncommon, but I'd expected something plainer. This one was well kept and a little high-end: two palm trees towered over a common area where blue-and-white-striped pool chairs surrounded three metal tables with matching umbrellas. A large woman wearing a yellow bathing cap was in the pool with what I guessed were her grandchildren splashing happily around her. A leathery old man lay nearly horizontal on a lounge recliner, glistening under a thick coat of suntan lotion, his skin as dark as an overripe banana.

"Up here," a voice called.

I looked up and saw Mac standing on the second floor walkway in front of his apartment, the door open behind him. "Did you bring your bathing suit?"

I couldn't tell if he was joking so I didn't say anything. I waved, found the stairs and hurried up.

His apartment was a modest two-bedroom; one room had been turned into an office with a desk, filing cabinets and a small table with one chair. He gave me a quick tour, lingering at the bedroom door. I stood next to him in the doorframe and poked my head in. A king-sized bed took up most of the space. A dark wood dresser lined one wall with a mirror conveniently providing a wide-angle view of the bed. Whatever he did in there could be viewed in the mirrored glass.

"I'd invite you in," he said, meaning the bedroom, "but we may never leave, so let's save the bedroom for next time. Bring a toothbrush."

*Next time. Bring a toothbrush. God help me.*

He led me back into the living room. There was a marble-topped island kitchen with a stove beyond it and four stools pressed up around the counter. A large, dark brown couch faced a front window that looked out onto the courtyard below. Sheer cream drapes fluttered in the breeze; apparently Mac liked it on the cold side, considering it was still winter.

There was a small gas fireplace perpendicular to the couch, a coffee and two end tables, and a television in an entertainment center that included a stereo and cassette player. I became aware of a piano softly playing classical music.

"Chopin?" I asked. My mother, who had become a faded memory for me, had loved the composer.

"Nocturne in E Flat Major," he said.

I nodded as if I'd known it.

"You like Chopin?"

"It reminds me of my mother," I said. "She died from breast cancer when I was sixteen."

"I'm sorry."

"Don't be. Everybody dies."

I winced at my own words. It wasn't the sort of thing you should say to a man you wanted to keep seeing.

He seemed to know it came from feelings I was not prepared to discuss.

"Have a seat, Marshall. Can I get you something to drink? Coffee? Soda?"

"Coffee would be good. If it's already made … don't go to any trouble."

"None at all." He headed to the counter by the stove where I could see a half full pot of coffee tucked in a machine.

He made a cup for me with his back turned. I took the opportunity to look more closely around the room. On the entertainment center I saw a photograph of Mac and another man. They stood closer than friends usually do, and when I walked over to examine it more carefully I saw they were holding hands. Mac was several years younger in the photograph, perhaps a decade. Hot as hell, as was the man next to him: a half foot taller than Mac, short sandy hair, set jaw, and laughing eyes that peered at the camera above a wide smile.

"That's Bobby," he said, having walked up behind me with my cup of coffee. "Bobby Learned. Great last name, and fitting. He was a very knowledgeable man."

I jumped; I hadn't heard him coming.

"You were a couple?" I asked.

"The love of my life, if you want the truth. I always

prefer it."

"Of course. Truth ... with a dash of discretion." I turned around, took the coffee from him and walked to the couch. We both sat down.

"Bobby was murdered six years ago," he told me. "It's what got me into homicide."

It was my turn to say I was sorry.

He did not say, 'Everybody dies.' Cynicism wasn't his way. Instead he said, "I didn't think I would survive that. We lived together in Beachwood Canyon. We had a house, it was wonderful."

I waited for him to go on.

"One night Bobby was getting into his car by the Beverly Center—I never knew why he'd parked on the street. That was just something he did. He didn't like parking garages. It was a phobia." He laughed lightly. "Isn't that weird, the quirks we have?"

He turned away, haunted by painful memories.

"Somebody mugged him. Shot him. Black guy? White guy? Woman? Who knows? Nobody saw anything. A couple people heard him shout, then a gunshot, then nothing."

"On a crowded street?" I asked, surprised.

"Maybe that worked against him. All I knew was that there were no reliable witnesses, no evidence besides a shell casing for a .45. It's still in storage in a cold-case box downtown. I know the case number, the evidence tag number, all the numbers that made up his life, including the one that mattered most: one shot, through the chest."

He looked at me and I could see years of sadness in his eyes, as if it had settled there and refused to leave. It was the first time I'd noticed something about him that would become a defining feature.

"We were just kids, really. Mid-twenties. Happy. *Out*. That was saying a lot back then. You come out on the police force today and it can be tough, but ten years ago when we first met? He always told me how proud he was of me for being open about us. But I didn't have a choice, you know? I couldn't be that happy and not *live* it."

"Was he was a cop, too?" I asked quietly.

"Oh, God no. He sold life insurance. How's that for irony? Anyway, they never caught the mugger. The insurance company paid me twenty-five thousand dollars, as if that settled it. I advanced from a beat cop to a homicide detective in record time—call me motivated. I still hope the gun used to shoot him turns up someday, gets traced back to that shell casing, and I can look the bastard in the eye right before I kill him."

He saw the alarm on my face. "I don't really mean it. I'm a cop. We don't kill people unless we have to." He smiled. "But maybe he could be provoked into doing something stupid. Call it self-defense, one more piece of shit off the streets, everybody's happy."

"I had no idea this was part of your life."

"How could you? I didn't know about your mother until today."

"I can deal with death," I said. "It's all around us now—I went to four memorials last year—but not murder."

My own words struck me. I was wrong. Murder was very much around me, at least the last two days.

"I have to tell you something," I said.

He slid his hand onto my thigh. "Go ahead, I'm listening."

"I knew the second victim, too. Freddy Carpenter."

"Really?"

"Well, I didn't *know* him, but he was a regular at the Parrot and, I'm assuming, the Red River, since his dismembered body was found there. I also saw him at the baths."

"When?"

"About a half hour before you showed up in my doorway."

He withdrew his hand, thinking about what I'd told him. "I wonder if that's where he met the killer."

The thought chilled me. If the man who killed Ben also

killed Freddy, and if he'd been at the baths at the same time we all were, it meant I may know him, at least by sight.

"Speaking of the killer," I said. "How did a reporter for the Blaze know there were unopened bottles of poppers in the victims' shirt pockets?" These were details Mac would know as part of the homicide team but that should not have been released to the public. "Don't you guys keep these things secret, in case you get crazy people confessing to crimes they didn't commit?"

"The police department leaks, I hate to break it to you. I don't know the source of that information but my superiors are aware of it. Giving out details like that can hurt an investigation."

"And give the media something to call this maniac, like *Popper Jack*. It can start a panic in the bars. I don't think we're there yet, but I see it coming."

"I've been assigned to a task force," he said. "That's all I'll say about it, but trust me, we're determined to stop whoever is doing this."

"Be careful," I said. "Considering how leaky the department is, he might see you coming."

"I'm always careful," he said, smiling. "Can we change the subject now?"

"To what?"

He slid his hand between my legs. "I invited you here for lunch, but there may not be time."

"What could possibly distract us?"

He pushed me gently down on the couch. With a quick glance at the window to make sure the drapes were pulled, he melted down on top of me and started unbuttoning my shirt.

# NINETEEN

A WEEK FEELS LIKE FOREVER when there's a killer on the loose. It didn't take long for the sketchy news reports to ignite full-fledged panic in the community. While the bars could be as different from each other as the people who drank in them, they all served a gay clientele and the friends who showed up with them. In places like the Paisley Parrot and the Red River, where drinking to excess was the objective, there weren't many straight girlfriends tagging along for a night out.

The reporter for the Blaze, apparently sensing his big break, ran with the story as if he were a young journalist at the LA Times and this was his ticket to a Pulitzer. I'd made note of his name: Brad Herring. He'd become familiar to all of us who read the paper and quite a few who'd never heard of it until the shocking murders it shamelessly exploited for ad revenue. Popper Jack was now a celebrity with the sort of dubious fame reserved for psychopaths and mass murderers—titles he could legitimately claim if the murders were the work of one man.

"Of course it's one person," Phil said, wiping the bar down on a Tuesday night. "The poppers alone make that clear. He's leaving a signature."

"But maybe he had help," said a customer, propping himself up with an elbow and a third gin fizz. "Sometimes these monsters work in pairs."

"Gacy didn't need help," Phil responded, referring to the infamous serial killer John Wayne Gacy who turned Chicago into his personal hunting ground in the 1970s.

"Maybe it's a *she*," said a voice down the bar, an exceptionally short old man who was known for his inebriated efforts to enchant people with stories of the Parrot's glory days, when you might spot Rock Hudson at a back booth or Paul Lynde groping some young thing by the pool table. "Maybe it's one of those bitter dykes from LuLu's who decided to take out forty years of rage on the nearest queen."

I'd kept my mouth shut and just listened. This was the kind of wild speculation burning through the bars, and it had only been eight days since poor Freddy Carpenter was found butchered.

Looking back on it, I believe some of the panic, some of the *excitement*, came from simply having something besides AIDS to think about, something killing us that could be stopped, apprehended, *stared in the face*. Death, for us and those we knew, had become a presence, a man in a darkened doorway who never came out of the shadows but who called to us, one by one.

Popper Jack was real and immediate. He had a name, he had a body that would be revealed when the police paraded him in handcuffs or they put his picture on TV next to a body bag. We could fight this; we were not helpless, and it made all the difference.

* * *

We watched the news first thing each morning, expecting to see another victim found behind one of the bars with no new leads for the cops to follow. First one day passed, then another. By the weekend, despite rising panic among the bar goers, I'd begun to secretly hope the nightmare had moved on—that the killer had achieved whatever satisfaction he was after and left town to claim his prizes in some other hapless community. People came and went constantly in Hollywood. There was no reason to think a murderer might not also be as transient. Maybe he was a travelling salesman, or a truck driver. Maybe he wasn't even from this country and had visited his wickedness upon us during his winter holiday from Eastern Europe. These were possible, if implausible, scenarios, and each of us clung to our own versions, waiting for the storm to pass at the same time we anticipated another lightning strike.

I'd spent exactly one more night with Mac, on his day off. He hadn't offered me any information than wasn't already available. I knew he wouldn't divulge details even if he could. He was taking an enormous risk dating me—for that is how I saw it by then, we were dating—and I couldn't ask him to compound that risk by telling me what the police knew about the killings.

We had not discussed his murdered lover again. He offered nothing more about the handsome, doomed Bobby Learned, and I didn't ask. For all the differences gay men want to think we have from our straight counterparts, we're still *men,* still subject to the cultural pressures and assumptions placed on us from the moment some obstetrician in a delivery room shouts, "It's a boy!" We keep things to ourselves. We hold our emotions in check. We don't cry, and we seldom talk about it. Mac would open up when and if he wanted to, just as I might someday talk about my mother, her death, and the shell of a drunken husband she left behind to blight his children. These were possibilities for a future well removed from the immediate realities of dead victims and a serial killer with a catchy nickname.

At that point in time all of us were grateful to still be alive, despite the anxiety of not knowing when the Grim Reaper might knock on the door and refuse our demand that he go away. Death came quickly for us then, like a shadow sliding over us, and when it passed we were gone.

By Friday night I'd let my guard down. The bar traffic had slowed noticeably—I assumed more people were drinking at home or in small groups until the terror of Popper Jack left us in its wake. I'd just served a customer his usual scotch and water when I looked to my left and saw a man settling onto the next stool. He was unfamiliar to me, not something that happened often at the Parrot. Few people found themselves there by accident (Ben had been a glaring exception). It was the kind of place you went to out of habit and for the comfort of a barstool that knew the weight of your body from long acquaintance.

He wasn't especially handsome. He had wavy, brushed-back brown hair that looked in the dim light like it needed to be washed three days ago. Could be jell, could be lax hygiene. His fingers were pudgy and short, and he wore a single silver band on his right hand. I wondered if he was married. Sometimes married men moved their wedding rings to their right hands in a not-too-successful attempt to hide the fact.

"What can I get you?" I said.

You can smell alcohol on someone's breath even in a bar. You might think this wasn't the case, given the cloud of smoke and the booze-soaked atmosphere, but alcohol released through the lungs has a distinct, living odor to it. I could tell he'd already had a few drinks before he came in.

"Scotch, neat," he said, his speech slurred. He winked at me.

*Seriously*? I thought. *He's loaded at six o'clock, in a bar he's never been to before, and he's hitting on me*? I couldn't decide whether to be flattered or repulsed.

I got the man his drink and set it on a coaster in front of him. As I drew my hand away, he dropped a business card on the bar between us: *The Blaze,* it said in big, bold print beneath the paper's logo. And beneath that: *All the Gay News You Can Use*. Below that was the name *Brad Herring* and a phone number.

"I'd like to talk to you," he said, seeming more sober than I'd thought he was.

"You don't know who I am," I replied, and it was true. I hadn't offered my name.

"Oh, I know everything. How long this place has been here, the types of queers who like it ... *who really owns it*. And it's not that stooge Oscar LeGrand, if he's even still alive. I hear he's in a landfill."

When he said who really owned the bar, he meant Fat Dick and the mob. "I have nothing to do with the business side. I'm just a bartender."

"'Just'?" he said. "I think you're more than that, Marshall James. I think you're witness to a murder."

"I found a body. That hardly makes me a witness. And what you did to poor Freddy Carpenter is inexcusable."

"You mean telling my readers what people like you already knew and only his wife wasn't aware of? I believe that was up to Freddy, and he chose the coward's way."

"He has two children."

"Who have to grow up sooner or later. I always think sooner is the better choice."

I leaned toward him and said, "I don't know you, don't like you, and don't expect either of those to change. Now, if you don't mind …"

I started to turn away. He reached out and grabbed my hand. "I think the victims would mind, Mr. James. I think their loved ones would mind, regardless of what they knew or didn't know about these men." He looked around the bar, indicating the dozen patrons we had at the time. "I think the gay community would mind very, very much."

He let my hand go and I stayed there, not knowing why. Guilt, I suppose, the feeling that I owed it to Ben and Freddy and even Mac to talk to this sleazy reporter. Maybe he wasn't the only one who could learn something from the encounter. I doubted there was much I could offer Brad Herring, but there might be something he could tell me, if just in a slip of the tongue.

"When and where do you want to talk?" I asked. "Not here, that's for sure."

"Afraid you'll be accused of sleeping with the enemy?"

"We'll never sleep together, and you're not the enemy. You're a reporter without a conscience. You can stick around till closing, or come back at two o'clock and we'll go someplace. If you stay, I'd suggest pacing yourself. You've had a few already and there's no point talking if you're loaded."

He picked up his glass and finished it in a swallow. "I'll

come back," he said, winking again.

I took the ten dollar bill he'd laid on the counter and walked off to make change. When I headed back from the cash register he was gone.

* * *

Herring was a man of his word. Just when I thought I'd never see him again, sometime around a quarter to two, he walked in past the door curtain, unsteady but not at the falling down stage. The only customers remaining that close to last call were the diehards and the desperate, and a few who were both.

"Hey," I said, nodding at him as he stumbled up to the bar. "You made it."

"I have a reputation to maintain," he said. "You remember what I like?"

"In what regard?"

He mimed sipping a drink.

"Scotch, hold the water," I said. "How could I forget? You ordered it with a wink. But are you sure you want another? Where'd you have all the ones between then and now?"

"Red River," he said. "There was a second murder there if you recall. And I'm fine. I just look a little shaky. Make it a double."

I wasn't sure what to think of this guy. He couldn't have been much older than me, maybe thirty, but he drank like somebody who'd been at it awhile. Maybe he'd started early in life like a lot of us. Being gay in a society that doesn't like you can have you easing the pain with booze and pills when most kids are still figuring out their college major.

"Where are you from?" I asked, setting his drink on top of a coaster.

"Michigan. And you?"

"Indiana."

"Neighbors!" He lifted his glass in a toast only he was

making and threw back half his drink.

"Gruesome situation," he said, putting the glass down.

"Growing up in Indiana?"

"I like your sense of humor, James."

I saw Phil watching us from the other end of the bar. I waved: everything's okay. He nodded and went back to cleaning up. We'd be locking up in a half hour, provided we could herd the last few drunks out the door.

"Come again?" I asked, not having paid attention.

"I was talking about that Red River business. I was over there chatting up the bartender, the one who found Freddy Carpenter in sections."

"That's why you're here," I said. "You want to pump me for information."

"If you insist." He finished his drink and tapped the table for another one. "Let's have a conversation, shall we? Fix us both something and I'll just go take a piss, back in a flash."

He poured himself off the barstool and wobbled toward the bathroom. I'd planned on talking somewhere else, but it was already halfway to tomorrow and nobody was around to hear us anyway. Phil didn't count. I got myself a Jack and Coke, finished half of it and waited for our Q & A.

* * *

Everyone was gone by the time Brad Herring walked out of the Paisley Parrot. Phil had left around two-thirty when it was just him, me, Herring and a dapper old gentlemen named Victor who was known to wear a suit and tie every day of his life, even though he'd retired years ago and the only office he went to was a bar. We knew Victor from his years at the Parrot; he predated all of us, and while we sometimes worried he'd die from old age and not be found for a week, we knew he could manage to get himself off the stool, out the door and up the street to his apartment.

Finally even Victor was gone, and I stared at Herring

through my own whiskey haze. I'd meant to take it easy, but the past week had been rough. I felt entitled to overdo it that night.

I'd told Herring the same things I'd told the police and Mac. I didn't have more details, and I didn't tell Herring about seeing Freddy at the baths. It was surely a coincidence—I'd seen Freddy there many times—and could only fuel useless speculation from a reporter looking for more sensation.

"You didn't write any of this down," I said. "Don't reporters write things down?"

"This," he said, tapping his temple with a finger. "This is my recorder. I see all, hear all, and remember all. You're from Indiana …"

"Right."

"You had a man crush on this guy, Bennig …"

"Wennig."

"Yeah, Ben Wennig, whose body you found in the dumpster right back there—" He pointed at the back door.

"That is correct."

"And now you're fucking the lead detective."

"*What*? Where did you hear that?"

He shrugged, then drew a zipper across his lips.

"Let me guess," I said. "From the same source who's been feeding you information from the Department. Nobody knew about the poppers in the victims' pockets until you printed it. It's a terrible name, by the way, 'Popper Jack.' Most people don't even know what poppers are."

"Most people don't read the Blaze. But it caught on, didn't it? That's what all the news outlets are calling him now. I'm good at my job, what can I say?"

"So why sit here drinking with me? You already know everything I've told you."

"The story's cold," he said, frustrated. He held up his glass for another and I shook my head no, he'd had more than enough. "I need a new angle."

"Is that what people are to you, Brad? Angles?"

He stared at me. "Aren't they just another drink to you, Mr. High-and-Mighty bartender? You think telling people's stories for a living is any less honorable than selling them another glass of despair?"

"You're a poet, too," I said.

"And great sex."

"I think we're done here," I said. I took his glass and dropped it into the dish pan under the counter.

"Okay, okay, sorry. I get it. I'm a sleazy reporter, he's a hot cop. I can't blame you. But I just wonder … this killer is someone you've seen. Maybe someone you know."

"I don't think so," I said unconvincingly.

"He'd probably ordered a drink from you earlier that night. Hell, maybe you've had sex with him and just got lucky."

"Lucky?" I said, appalled.

"You're alive, aren't you?"

I'd had enough of Brad Herring. The conversation was getting uncomfortable for me. Of course I'd thought about the killer sitting on the same bar stool Herring was on now. And cruising the baths, and walking the streets of Hollywood, smiling, waving at people who knew him but would never imagine him as a serial killer.

"I need to finish up here and go home," I said. "This discussion has provided little new information for you, and nothing of interest for me."

"Except that I know things."

"It's your job. Which you do best when you're sober, like the rest of us. So go home, Brad, and sleep it off. You need a taxi?"

"I'm fine," he said. "Give me your number and I'll get out of this dump." He took another business card out of his wallet and handed it to me with a pen.

"I have a boyfriend," I said. "But you knew that already."

"It's not for a date, although I'm tempted. I just might have some more questions."

Against my better judgment, I took the pen, wrote down my number and handed the card back to him.

He smiled, gave me an inebriated salute, then pushed his way out onto the sidewalk.

## TWENTY

I SLEPT LATE THE NEXT morning, but not well. I'd spent most of the night battling dreams from which I'd struggled my way to consciousness every hour or so before falling back into darkness. It was like coming up for air, or being disturbed by a sudden shaft of light in an otherwise black room, then having the light vanish again as I disappeared into the nothingness of sleep.

When I finally managed to keep my eyes open, I saw on the nightstand clock that it was almost noon. It was rare for me to sleep five hours, let alone a full eight, and I jumped out of bed as if the day was half gone. I looked at my answering machine, hoping to see a flashing light with a message from Mac. We hadn't spoken in two days and I was worried he'd already lost interest. There was no logical reason for me to think this, it's just what happens when we're in the infatuation stage. He was hot, he was a cop, he was older … there was nothing missing from this picture except a lifetime commitment.

I'd grabbed my pager to see if he'd buzzed me, when the phone rang. It startled me, rattling on the nightstand like an unwanted alarm. I snatched it out of the cradle, hoping it was Mac.

"Hello?" I said, as eager as a puppy for his master's voice.

"They found another one." No introduction, no effort to verify the caller had dialed the right number.

"Phil?" I replied. I knew his voice immediately. It had a smoky quality to it, probably from the two packs of cigarettes he smoked every day.

"Yeah, Marshall, it's me. I didn't know if you'd seen it on the news yet."

"I just woke up, I haven't watched anything."

He expressed no surprise that I'd slept till noon. Phil probably didn't get up much earlier than that every day of his life.

"Get this," he said, "it's that reporter."

I felt my stomach tighten into a fist. "What reporter?" I asked, already knowing the answer.

"The one from the Blaze. The one who was at the bar last night, *talking to you*."

"What the hell?"

"'What the hell' is right, Marshall. I'm surprised you didn't hear this from the cops by now. It can't be hard to figure out the guy's last moves."

"Excuse me, Phil, but you make it sound like I had something to do with this."

My words were greeted with a telling silence.

"Seriously?" I said. "C'mon, man, you were there."

*But I left you at 2:30 a.m., dude,* I could hear him thinking. *Alone with that reporter who's dead now.*

He said, unconvincingly, "Of course you didn't have anything to do with it. But you were probably the last one to see him alive."

"No," I corrected him. "Whoever killed him was the last one to see him alive."

"Right."

"What are the details, Phil? Did they offer any on the news?"

"Just that he was found naked in his living room, stabbed multiple times. That must have come from a paramedic, they're the first to drop a dime for a few bucks or a free meal."

He was right. Emergency personnel, maids, cops—they were all known to make a quick call to a gossip rag if they could divulge something worth a few bucks, or even just for the shock value.

My mind was racing. Brad Herring had *not* been murdered and left outside a bar to be found at sunrise. It was different this time. Ben had been strangled. I didn't know how Freddy died—he'd been taken apart and left in bags. Whatever the killer's MO, this was a departure for him, if it was the same man.

"Maybe it's not connected," I said hopefully.

"No, it's Popper Jack all right," said Phil. "His boyfriend found a bottle of poppers stuck in his mouth."

"Ah, jeez ... That information definitely came from someone who gets paid for the gory details."

"No. It came from the boyfriend. He's crying in front of every camera someone shoves at him. Julio is his name. He's a nurse or something on the night shift at Kaiser. Came home around six this morning to find his reporter boyfriend dead on the floor."

I grabbed my shirt from last night off the end of the bed where I'd tossed it. Talking to Phil, I checked the pocket for the card Brad Herring had given me when he'd first come into the Parrot.

"I think it's time to panic," I said.

Finding no card in my shirt, I yanked my jeans from the floor and quickly rifled through the pockets.

"Past time," Phil replied. "There's already flyers going up around the neighborhood and in the bars. Popper Jack is in big, bold letters on all of them. We're officially being hunted by a serial killer."

No card in my jeans, either. I scanned my memory and found an image of myself leaving Herring's business card by the cash register. I hadn't thought I would need it, and now it was useless, except as evidence he'd been at the Parrot alone with me. I knew the next phone call I made would be to Mac. This was careening out of control, turning into something that both involved me and was far beyond me.

"I need to go, Phil," I said. "Thanks for calling. You gonna be at the Parrot tonight?"

"I don't have much of a life outside that place," he said. "I'll see you there. And be careful, Marshall, you hear me? We all have to be."

I assured Phil I would be fine and extremely cautious,

then hung up and headed for the shower. I needed to rinse the fear off me with the hottest water I could stand.

From that moment on I kept one eye over my shoulder. The thought was inescapable that evil was watching and waiting for us.

# TWENTY-ONE

I HAD NO IDEA YOU could get from Glendale to Hollywood in fifteen minutes, but Mac pulled it off. I never asked if he used his lights and siren—he drove an unmarked detective's car that gave itself away by being like all the other unmarked cars. We'd learned to spot them a block away when we were hustling for supper and a couch to sleep on.

I'd taken a quick, nearly scalding shower and poured myself a second cup of coffee, this one black. I had the strange idea that black coffee was stronger, as if milk diluted the caffeine rush. The news of Brad Herring's murder had already saturated the local news channels. He was a reporter, after all, one of them no matter how ready they were to dismiss the Blaze and its gay readership. I listened to a couple reports, surfing between network affiliates. Then I hit the mute button, not wanting to hear the same few details repeated with minor variation from one station to the next.

*Brad Herring was last seen at the Paisley Parrot bar.* By whom? I wondered. *Brad Herring was found stabbed in his Van Ness Avenue apartment.* While the stabbing wasn't news to me, I wondered how he got home after leaving the bar. I'd assumed he'd taken a taxi, but where did the killer make contact with him, and how did he hail a cab? Taxis don't generally roam the streets in L.A. looking for pickups the way they do in New York. Had the killer offered him a ride? Even in his drunken state, I found it hard to imagine him getting into a car with a stranger. *So the killer's not a stranger. Think about that, Marshall.* I'd begun to think about it a lot, peering at customers and wondering if one of them was at the bar looking for his next victim.

*Herring's body was discovered by his roommate, Julio*

*Dominguez*. Ah, yes, the roommate. It was 1983, we were still in the habit of calling gay lovers 'roommates.' But Julio was obviously more than that, displaying his intense grief and shock for any reporter spelling his name correctly. *Is the murder connected to the recent slew of killings in Hollywood's gay community? Has Popper Jack struck again?* That last one threw me. I didn't know two murders were a slew, and I was dismayed to hear the name Popper Jack being used now by all the media. Could Geraldo Rivera be far behind, pursuing some investigative piece about a killer of homosexuals who would be forgiven by people who thought we deserved it? AIDS was already being called God's vengeance. Maybe God needed a sidekick named Popper Jack to kill the strays.

I was contemplating a third cup of coffee when my pager went off. It was Mac, sending me a number to call. We hadn't discussed the whole pager thing long enough to set up any system. Back then you could only transmit numeric messages on most pagers used by the public. But you could still create codes, such as '4357' for 'HELP', or, in this case, a number to call.

I dialed the number. Answering, he said, "I'm in a phone booth a block away. Meet me downstairs in three minutes."

My apartment hadn't had a working intercom for months. All of the tenants complained, but the building manager didn't care and the landlord was a phantom.

"See you soon," I said. I hung up and hurried down four flights of stairs to the front door.

We'd been seeing each other for less than two weeks, long enough for us to know we had feelings for each other but still so new the sight of him made my breath catch. I could see him through the front door glass. He was wearing a red windbreaker I hadn't seen before. Jeans, gray tennis shoes, and a beige golf shirt. No suit. Was it his day off? Did that mean he could spend the day with me?

I composed myself coming down the last three steps. Another murder had been committed; this was not the time for imagining afternoons in bed with the hottest cop I had ever seen.

Ten minutes later we were sitting on my couch. I'd never given much thought to the condition of my apartment or how I'd decorated it, which was New American Sparse. I didn't place importance on objects, then or now, and aside from the usual, necessary sticks of furniture—a stereo, TV, and some posters on the wall—the place still looked like I'd just moved in after three years.

"Nice apartment," he said, glancing around.

It hit me: this was the first time Mac had been in my home. We'd had sex a half dozen times (counting our night at the baths as three of them), and I'd been at his apartment twice, but he hadn't come here.

"It needs work," I said.

When he turned back to look at me, his expression had darkened.

"I know about Brad Herring."

I froze. "The reporter for the Blaze. What do you know about him?"

"I saw the crime scene, Marshall ..."

I gasped.

"I'm off today," he continued, indicating his clothing.

*He hadn't told me he wasn't working today. Was that a bad sign?*

Reading my mind he said, "It was unexpected. My sister's kid was in a car accident and she called me last night."

I didn't know he had a sister, or that his sister had a kid. There was very little I knew know about Mac McElroy, and that lack of knowledge suddenly bothered me.

"Is he okay?"

"*She*. My niece's name is Stephanie and she's fine. My sister Carolyn just wanted the support, so I was going to Van Nuys this morning. I was planning to tell you about it when we spoke. Then the Department called and twenty minutes later I'm in Brad Herring's apartment at six o'clock in the morning."

"Herring was at the Parrot last night," I said, by way of heading off any sense of concealment.

"We know that."

*Not 'I' know that. 'We' know that. This wasn't just about me and Mac anymore.*

"Your name and home number were on one of his business cards on the coffee table, along with a pack of matches from the Paisley Parrot. The unopened bottle of poppers was in his mouth. Considering he was naked, it was the easiest place for the killer to put it."

"And you think the killer was me?" I said.

"Of course not. But I'm not the only one on this investigation."

"What are you telling me, Mac?"

He took a deep breath, then reached for my hand. "I can't protect you and don't want to, insofar as obstructing anything. The personal and the professional can get easily obscured here, Marshall."

"I wouldn't expect you to protect me! I don't have anything to hide. And I'm in as much danger as the rest of us. The killer goes to the bar, Mac! That seems clear now. I gave Herring my phone number when he came to see me. He wanted to talk to about the murders."

"It was bound to draw attention to you, sitting on a table next to a corpse."

"As if I needed more people interested in me." I was visibly agitated by that point. "Listen, he gave me his business card, I gave him my phone number. It's the only exchange of personal information that happened, and I left it at the Parrot on the bar, or maybe by the cash register. I had no intention of speaking to him again. I'd never met the guy until last night."

"I believe you, I hope you know that." He let my hand slip from his. "But this is how it has to be for a while. I can't be seen involved with a suspect."

"So that's what I am now, a suspect? That didn't take

long."

"It took three dead bodies, Marshall. Three innocent men who lost their lives in the most terrifying ways imaginable."

"And you think they're connect to me because I served them all drink?"

"I don't think that at all," he said, sighing loudly. "I'm doing this as much to help you—"

"As to hurt me?" I interrupted, immediately regretting my words.

"As to preserve the integrity of the investigation. Someone is murdering gay men and we have to stop it before he finds another victim."

"Another victim connected to me."

"Connected to you or the Parrot or anything else they have in common. I have to be seen as clean, please understand that. If they think I'm giving you information it would be a disaster for both of us."

He was right and I knew it.

"I can't stay long," he said. "My trip to my sister's house is going to be short, just for some support, then I'll be back at Homicide. But before I go, I want to set up a few code words so we can communicate with the pagers."

"Sure," I said. "Like 'HELP' and 'GOODNIGHT' for those wee hours when we're both getting off work and should be seeing each other but can't."

"Don't forget 'LOVE YOU,'" he added.

It was one of those *'Did I just hear that correctly?'* moments.

"Excuse me? What did you say?"

He took my hand again and looked into my eyes. "I have feelings for you, Marshall. *Those* kinds of feelings, and it was time I said it. And now I have to go, really, but I need to make love with you first."

*Those kinds of feelings. Make love ... what strange parallel universe had I found myself in?*

My head was spinning as fast as my heart was

pounding. This man I'd known barely two weeks, this cop investigating murders I was somehow part of, had just told me he loved me, *and* that he had time for sex—excuse me, for *making love*—before going off to his sister's house with no guarantee when we'd see each other again.

"Let's go," he said, standing up and starting to strip.

"What about the pager codes?"

"We'll get to it, I promise," he said. "But first things first."

"Yes, Sir!" I said. "Am I under arrest?"

"I wouldn't joke about that," he replied. "Not yet anyway. Now come here."

My pants were off, my shirt was on, as he grabbed me and pulled me to him. I felt myself falling … falling into passion, falling into lust, and, God help me, falling into love.

## TWENTY-TWO

I HADN'T STOPPED THINKING ABOUT it since Mac left me exhausted on the couch, sweat-drenched in January, watching as he dressed within arm's reach. I don't mean his body, which met my standards of perfection in every way, and I don't mean his crooked smile as he beamed it at me while he buttoned his shirt. What I could not stop thinking about was what he had told me: *We can't see each other … for now.* Was I foolish to want a better definition of what that meant? Did it mean we couldn't talk on the phone? Would I be able to at least go to his apartment and stare at him through the window, once I'd climbed a ladder to the second floor? And what about the 'for now' part? At that moment, saying goodbye with the taste of his tongue in my mouth and the smell of his sex in my nostrils, 'for now' might as well have been forever.

I'd stood in my doorway watching him go, listening intently for the last faint sound of his footsteps. Then I had closed my door and leaned against it for several minutes, running through everything in my mind, especially the effect it was all having on my relationship with the man in charge of investigating these murders.

*Lock the door, always.*

*Right.* I heard Mac's warning in my head and quickly turned the deadbolt on my door. Who might be coming for me was the big question that had to be answered before anyone was safe. He had also quickly gone over some pager codes so we could at least page each other.

225563 meant CALLME. 4357 for HELP. And 56838 for

LOVEU.

Yes, he'd said it, and he had said it first.

"Are you sure you want to say that?"

He'd slid his palm down my chest. "I'm very sure. 5-6-8-3-8. It's crazy, but it's true."

That became our secret code ... 5-6-8-3-8. I've even thought of sharing it with Boo all these years later, but he's not the secret code type, and it belongs to me and Mac.

I was confused, frightened, and elated all at the same time. I took another shower, this one long, luxurious and filled with the immediate memories of Mac on top of me, then I dressed and headed for lunch. I planned to take my time with it, read the L.A. Times and the Blaze. Being a weekly paper, they wouldn't yet have a cover story about the killing of their own reporter. Then I might walk to Hollywood Boulevard and see what broken dreams I could find on the sidewalk, and finally to the Parrot. Things were heating up fast and I anticipated at least a few anxious customers worried we were all under attack, which we were in so many ways.

* * *

The Parrot was more alive at 5:00 p.m. than I had ever seen it. I'd thought the place might be empty, our patrons staying home behind locked doors or spending time in groups of three or four. Panic did that to people, especially when the danger had no face, no name, and deadly intentions. Instead, I walked into a frenzy of activity and a chorus of voices, all talking at the same time.

I saw Billy Greer from the Gay Center holding court mid-bar, surrounded by several men I'd seen but never spoken to beyond a casual greeting. He had a stack of flyers in his hand, each emblazoned with a hand-drawn blank face and the name Popper Jack in large bold letters beneath it. I couldn't read the text under the name, but I knew it would include a warning to the community and emergency phone numbers to contact the Center and the police.

I waved at Phil who looked beleaguered behind the bar, trying to maintain order as the crowd grew louder and more agitated.

"What's going on?" I asked a young man on the periphery. He was drinking a beer and trying to listen to Billy's speech about gay men being hunted like animals.

"They want us dead," he said over his shoulder, not turning to look at me.

"Who is 'they'?" I asked.

"The whole fucking world," he replied bitterly. "The government, the city, the church … all of them. And now this freak, Popper Fucking Jack. He's gotta be a preacher, right? A preacher or a politician. Aren't they all?"

I wasn't going to disagree with him, however ridiculous I thought his claims sounded.

"Excuse me," I said, squeezing past him to get behind the bar. "I work here."

"You're the one!" he said, causing me to freeze.

"I'm the one, what?"

"The guy who works here! The one who found the first body. You're famous."

"I just happened to be there, wrong place, wrong time," I said. "Now if you'll excuse me …"

I hurried over to Phil. He looked a little less stressed than when I'd walked in, only because the crowd had focused its attention on Billy, allowing Phil to step back and breathe.

"He's a fucking agitator," Phil said, nodding at Billy.

"Well, there's something to be agitated about," I replied. "Three people are dead, maybe more to come. These are scary times."

"Especially for you."

I was taken aback by his words.

"Maybe it's not the Parrot that has this shark circling the waters. Maybe it's you."

"That's as offensive as it is crazy," I said. "And it doesn't sit well with me."

"If you think it doesn't sit well with you, imagine how the Bianchis feel about it."

He glanced past me at the door located at the end of the bar. While it was considered the bar's office, it really belonged to Fat Dick and whoever among the Bianchis or their hangers-on he might have with him—we never questioned it, we just knew they were mob and we stayed out of the way.

"Is he in there?" I asked.

"Oh yeah," Phil replied. "And he's not alone."

"Another boy toy?"

"Not this time." Phil's expression grew dark. "He's got Victor Bianchi and Sal Romeo with him."

The names meant nothing to me, but I gathered from the way Phil said them these were dangerous men. They would have to be to close themselves behind a door with Fat Dick. The office wasn't that big.

"I take it they're not here for the skim," I said.

"God no. They're talking about what to do."

"About what?"

"About *this*!" He motioned at Billy and the crowd. "It's going to kill the business.

"Some nutcase is chopping up gay men and they're worried about the *business*?"

He shrugged. "The only loss that matters to these guys is a loss of money. You know that."

I hadn't known it, actually, but it was another of life's many hard lessons I would learn over the years.

Phil leaned in close to me and whispered, "I hear they put a hit out on him."

"On Fat Dick?"

"No, idiot, on Popper Jack."

"That's nuts. Who puts out a contract on a serial killer?"

"The Bianchis, that's who."

Just then the far door opened and out rumbled two men who looked like they'd stepped from a casting call for *The*

*Godfather*. I hadn't seen either of them before, but I was very familiar with the third man out: Richard 'Fat Dick' Montagano. It was highly unusual to see him in the light of day—in fact, it may have been a first for me. He followed the two men past us and out from behind the bar, saying nothing to Phil or me. I could feel the anger coming off them in waves as they marched outside.

Fat Dick wasn't a bad looking man, just too big for anyone's good, especially his own. Tallish, about 5′ 11″, brown eyes that could charm you one second and threaten you the next, a preternaturally white smile he most likely accomplished with bleach, and fat hands to go with his (so we were told) fat dick. He'd even hit on me when I was first coming around the Parrot. I'd said no as politely as I could; then, when he pressed the issue, I lied and told him I had a boyfriend back in Indiana. He knew I was lying—the boyfriend came without photographs, a name or conjugal visits, plus Dick saw me whoring around with other guys at the bar—but he let it go and hadn't made a pass at me since.

"Are they coming back?" I asked, watching Dick close the outer door behind them.

"Let's hope not," Phil said.

I suddenly became aware of the crowd again when Billy shouted, "Hand these out! Everybody! Every bar, every lamppost!"

The crowd squeezed in as one man after another took a handful of flyers and headed outside to canvas the neighborhood and warn the citizenry of a killer in our midst.

It made me think of Ben, Freddy, and Brad Herring, who I'd talked to less than twenty-four hours before. I walked over to the cash register, expecting to find Brad's business card.

It wasn't there. I kept looking, lifting a pile of receipts, then sliding a stack of coasters to the side, thinking it might be under them. Nothing.

"Did you see a business card here?" I asked Phil.

"No, not today. Whose card is it?"

That was odd. I'd put it by the cash register, I was sure of it. Josef didn't normally get rid of things he found from the night shift. I glanced in the tip jar, thinking he might have tossed the card in there. It was nowhere to be found.

"Whose card is it?" Phil repeated.

It startled me out of my daydream. I looked at Phil, and for reasons I still don't know to this day, I said, "Nobody's. A massage therapist who was in last night. I could use one."

"A therapist or a massage?"

"Both. It's no big deal, forget it."

I don't believe in a sixth sense, ghosts or clairvoyance, but something that day told me to drop the subject with Phil. The scene was off, the way you might look twice at a room you'd been in before and wonder what small thing was different about it. There was a difference that afternoon, but I didn't know what it was.

"Want a drink?" Phil asked, smiling.

Billy had led his army out the door and we were alone, an unusual state of being at the Parrot.

"Not this time," I said. "Maybe after shift."

"I'll be here."

Of course he would be, and if the previous half hour had been any indication, it was going to be a long night.

## TWENTY-THREE

ONCE THE CROWD LEFT WITH their flyers and their paranoid conspiracy theories, business never picked up. The four or five lushes who stayed behind became our only steady customers for the night, reinforced with a dozen others who came and went.

"You think it's like this over at the Red River?" I asked Phil sometime around 10:00 p.m.

"I think it's like this everywhere," he said. "People are scared. Who wants to risk ending up in a plastic bag after drinks with a stranger?"

"Or dead in their apartment. Don't forget the reporter."

"Can't forget him," he said with a smirk.

It was the usual staffing, just me and Phil and Brandon as our barback. On a night that slow one of us could have gone home, but I sensed we felt more comfortable as well as safer together. Phil had been chatting up Lorraine, one of the few women regulars, as she fueled up for the night on screwdrivers.

"What's that supposed to mean?" I asked, annoyed at his tone.

"Last night he was your pal."

"He wasn't my pal! I'd never met the man before. He was in here snooping. He needed fresh copy and figured he could get a good story off of me, maybe a lurid description. I wasn't interested."

"In him or his story?"

"Neither."

"And now it's too late."

"Yeah, well, getting killed can do that to you."

I was sour and sulking by then. I didn't like Phil's attitude, partly because I couldn't tell if he was serious. Did he honestly think I had something to do with Herring's death? With any of their deaths? Or did he just think I had something to hide? If that was the case, I wished he'd tell me whatever secrets he thought I was keeping.

"I'm going for a smoke," he said, just about 11:00 p.m. He didn't have to go outside for a cigarette, but we both used it as an excuse to get some air and leave the bar atmosphere behind for a few minutes.

We had three more hours to go. Cleanup wouldn't take long, considering how light our traffic had been. I'd be home by 3:00 a.m., alone, staring at my pager to see if Mac had sent me that 56838 yet. So far he hadn't, and I wasn't going to be the one to cross that line again—my heart was on the other side.

"Enjoy," I said to Phil's back. He was already heading out the side door.

About the same time Phil vanished outside, a guy named Reginald came in. I hadn't seen him for a long time and had assumed he was dead, one of the fallen who'd been disappearing in increasing numbers that year. At that point in our lives it was a safe assumption.

"Hey, Reggie!" I said, surprised by my own enthusiasm for a man I only knew as a rum and Coke.

"Hey …?"

He didn't remember my name.

"Marshall. Don't worry about it, it's been awhile."

Reggie looked good. Middle age had been kind to him, and he had the appearance of a tourist: dressed well in khakis and a blue button-down shirt. I even detected a tan, despite the dim lighting.

He took a stool near me, close to the end of the bar. "Phil in?" he asked.

"He's out back having a smoke," I said. "You can join him if you want."

"Nah, I gave it up six months ago."

"Good for you," I said. I thought of my pack of Marlboros sitting by the cash register. And that made me think of Brad Herring's missing business card.

"You okay?" he asked, seeing me drift away.

I turned my attention back to him. "Fine, I'm fine. Just remembering something. You want a cocktail?"

"Rum and Coke," he said, telling me what I already knew. Then he added, "Hey, it's crazy, all these killings, yeah?"

"Crazy is a good word for it." I made his drink and set it in front of him. "You been out of town? You look … I don't know, like you're visiting."

He took a swallow and savored it, as if it had been awhile since his last encounter with a drink. "Odd way to put it. I mean, what's a visitor look like?"

"Not a tourist, exactly. I guess you just look … healthy."

"Ah, yes. I look like I'm not from around here." He laughed. "You're sort of right about that. I've been in Bakersfield for the past six months."

"Bakersfield?" My surprise was genuine. Bakersfield was a place people left, not one they went to, and never for six months. "It has to be love. What else would keep you there?"

He blushed so deeply it showed through his tan. "Good guess, actually. I met a guy, speaking of crazy. He was from Bakersfield, lived there all his life, that kind of thing. Family he didn't want to leave. Mother in poor health. He wasn't moving here, so the mountain went to Muhammad … and now the mountain's back. Still a little heartbroken, but the rum helps."

"I'm surprised you didn't run into Phil there," I said. "Maybe it's not that small of a town."

"Phil?" he said. "We've stayed in touch, talk every few weeks on the phone."

I had not known Phil and Reggie were friends. But there was a lot I didn't know about Phil and almost nothing I knew about Reggie.

"I would've known if he was in Bakersfield," he continued. "And, I mean, what the hell for? Did he meet some heartbreaking asshole, too?"

"No, his mother lives there."

He stared at me, his brow furrowed while he searched his memory. "Seriously? His mother?" He finished his drink and tapped the bar with his finger. I quickly refilled his glass. "Who told you that?"

"Phil told me. But maybe I misunderstood," I said instead.

"Yeah, man. Phil's mother lives in Phoenix. I met her a couple years ago when she was here visiting him. I kind of doubt she moved to Bakersfield, but you never know."

I heard the side door open and looked over as Phil came back in.

"We can ask him," Reggie said.

"No, that's okay," I said quickly, shaking my head. "I got it wrong, that's all, no big deal."

It was a big deal, but not one I would bring up to Phil directly at that point. He had lied about his mother living in Bakersfield, which meant he'd either lied about going there or lied about his reason for doing it. Something was very wrong with this picture and I did not want to examine it in Phil's presence.

"Look who's here!" I said loudly to Phil as he walked up to us behind the bar. I wanted to make sure Reggie dropped our conversation. "All the way from Heartbreak Hotel. Check your bags, Mr. Reggie?"

He looked at me like I was a nutcase, then shrugged it off and stood from his stool, leaning across the bar to hug Phil.

I eased away, leaving the two friends to get caught up. It was now 11:30 and an end to the evening was nowhere in sight. I needed to think, to examine the puzzle pieces I had in front of me and imagine how they fit together. I also had to stay alive, something my chances of doing seemed to decrease by the day.

## TWENTY-FOUR

PARANOIA MAKES YOU TWITCH. It invades your dreams. I spent what seemed like an eternity that night trying to outrun a shadow in a nightmare: I was lost in Hollywood, running down streets with no street signs. I remember looking up at them and seeing blurred black letters that looked as if they'd been smeared, deliberately disfigured to confuse and mislead me. I heard footsteps—his footsteps—catching up to me in the night. There were no street lights, either; this dream world was exclusively, distinctly, dark. I found myself turning corners, one after the other, before I realized I was being chased in a tightening spiral toward a terrifying end. And then I got there ... no more corners to turn, no more streets to flee down. I remember being surprised at how bright this place was, this deadly center of a dream, before looking up to see a full moon bathing my nightmare in a vast, pale light. I heard those last few footsteps. I turned, and I saw his face ...

I sat upright as if I'd been punched in the gut. My sheet was damp from sweat and stuck to me in the early morning coolness. I looked around the room, forcing its familiar objects into focus as a way to yank myself fully awake. I was not on a nameless street in the middle of a dream. I was in my bed, in a *real* world that was fast becoming indistinguishable from a nightmare. Someone was killing men, someone who knew me ... someone *I knew*. I was both victim and suspect, lover and threat, known and unknown. I tried to remember the man I'd seen in my dream, but all I recalled was the shock of it. I didn't know who this killer was; how could I expect to recognize his face?

I glanced at the clock. It was almost 10:00 a.m. I'd slept straight through for seven hours, and while the sleep had been disturbed by a terror still clinging to my mind, it had been uninterrupted. No tossing and turning, no leaps into and out of consciousness. It had been weirdly rejuvenating, and as I slid out of bed to start my day, I felt drained yet refreshed. My body had rested while my mind had been chased through a dreamscape.

I wanted to call Mac but couldn't. I thought of paging him, but the more I'd thought about the whole situation, the more I wanted to leave him alone—to stay away from him—as a way of protecting him. Who knew where this would end? Who knew where *I* would end? *Possibly in a bag somewhere, or as an innocent man on death row.* Stop it Marshall, I told myself. Believe that this will turn out right, that you'll survive, that Ben and Freddy and Brad will have justice.

Standing in my kitchen listening to the percolator, knowing I could not call Mac, I thought of someone I could reach out to. A comforting friend, a steady hand. I left the coffee pot brewing and went into the living room. Sitting on the couch, I took the phone and dialed, expecting to leave a message this late in the morning.

"Hello?" Butch said.

I didn't respond immediately. I was surprised to hear him pick up the phone—to be at home when he should have left hours ago for his office.

"Butch?" I said.

"Marshall, who the hell else would answer my phone? I live alone with a cat and she isn't talking. What's up?"

"Why are you home?"

He sighed, then said, "This is why you call me? To ask me why I'm home?"

That was when I heard it: the weariness in his voice, a distinct hoarseness. It was the other thing that had surprised me when he'd answered. He sounded tired.

"Are you okay?"

"I'm not answering anymore questions until you answer mine."

"Someone's killing gay men. I'm a gay man. Does that

help?"

That got his attention.

"Butch, I know this sounds crazy, but I think this killer, Popper Jack, comes to the bar. That I know him."

"Don't you think you'd be dead if he was interested in you?"

"I don't know what I think," I said. "And I can't call Mac. It's a long story." I paused, then asked, "Can I come tell it to you, Butch?"

I'd assumed he would say yes, that he would jump at the chance to see his old friend. Instead he hesitated. "The timing's not great," he said.

"Are you going out? Could I meet you somewhere?"

He paused and sighed even deeper. Something was wrong. "Sure, Marshall. Come on over. We should talk anyway."

It was the second time that morning I'd felt like a fist had been shoved into my stomach. It wouldn't be the last.

We ended our conversation in another minute or two and hung up. I could get to Butch's place in less than an hour, with coffee, a shower and shave in between. The dread I'd felt in my dream returned as I got ready to leave. I had the feeling I knew exactly what was coming when I left my apartment to see Butch.

* * *

"You can say I look like shit," Butch said, letting me into his apartment. "Anything else is a lie, and lies are for people with time on their hands."

I'd been stunned when he opened the door still in his bathrobe. He'd obviously bathed. His hair was wet and combed back, but he hadn't shaved. Stubble covered his face … a thinner face than I'd seen the last time. It's hard for people now to imagine how quickly we deteriorated in those days, how suddenly we vanished. There were many weeks when someone I knew was alive on Monday and dead on

Friday. Combined with the physical depletion, the exhaustion that AIDS visited upon the flesh, he looked as if he'd been shoved into a wringer and come out the other side still alive.

"What's going on?" I asked, immediately thinking the question was pointless. We both knew what was going on.

"The Hollywood diet," he said, leading me to the couch where he sat and motioned me to join him. A large glass ashtray sat on the coffee table, a half dozen cigarette butts mashed into its center.

"You're smoking again," I said. Butch had stopped a year ago.

"What's that saying from those war movies? 'Smoke 'em if you got 'em'? Kind of applies to my situation."

"You know this from a doctor?" I asked, taking my own pack of cigarettes out of my shirt pocket. Normally I wouldn't smoke in his apartment but there didn't seem any point in resisting.

He rolled his eyes at me. We knew as much about the disease as most doctors did, and we were very effective at self-diagnosis: lesions meant Kaposi's sarcoma; night sweats, rapid weight loss, Pneumocystis pneumonia, meant you had the plague—or the plague had you. All the doctors did was tell us what we already knew.

Butch took a matchbook and lit a Kool from his near-empty pack. I noticed the Paisley Parrot's logo. "Nice timing," he said, seeing me eye the matches. "You're here to talk about the murders, right?"

"I was, yes, but …"

"Then you get a look at me in the doorway and you think I'd rather talk about being infected." He stared hard at me. "You're wrong."

I took a deep breath, then lit a cigarette of my own. "Fine, Butch, but we will talk about it."

He shrugged: maybe we would, maybe we wouldn't.

"For now, yes, I'm here about the killings. Three so far, and I knew all of the victims."

His eyes shot up; this was news to him.

"I didn't know them well," I said quickly. "And Ben—the first one—was the only one I slept with. Freddy I only knew from serving him drinks at the Parrot, and Brad Herring, the reporter, I talked to once, the night he was killed."

"And you think it's too much for coincidence. Have you told the authorities? Or at least the one you're sleeping with?"

I felt myself blushing. "Mac and I are on hold, for the time being. He's the lead investigator— "

"And you're the investigated. I understand. That must be hard."

"It is. But there's more."

He took another drag and blew a cloud of smoke out into the room. "I'm waiting …"

"You know Phil, the bartender?"

"Hot body, tattoos, bald."

"That's the one."

"I hear he's into leather," he said, and there was an unfamiliar gleam in his eye. We can be friends with someone and still be surprised by the things they do behind closed doors.

"I can't speak to that," I said. "But I have this idea … it's crazy I know, but … I'm worried he's involved somehow."

I felt fur brush against my ankles and jumped. Butch's cat, Lurline, had silently appeared and decided to weave her way between my feet. I reached down without looking and petted her.

"She's needy," Butch said, smiling. "Like her human companion. Go on …"

"I'm sure one thing's not connected to another, but Phil took off the night Ben Wennig was killed. He said he had to go to Bakersfield to help his mother. She'd sprained her ankle or twisted her leg, something like that. Then, last night, this guy he'd dated awhile back, Reggie, shows up when Phil was out back smoking. Turns out Reggie lives in

Bakersfield now. I mentioned Phil's trip …"

"Let me guess. The trip was a lie."

"Yes. Or at least the destination was. Reggie said he knew Phil's mother, and she lives in Phoenix."

"Maybe she moved to Bakersfield," he said. "Can't you just ask him?"

The cat must have felt ignored. She gave my leg one more rub, then sauntered into the kitchen. I could hear her nibbling dry food out of a bowl.

"If I ask and she moved, he'll think I don't trust him. And if she didn't move he'll know something's up, that I suspect him."

"You have to tell Mac."

I crushed out my cigarette. "I will, when I have something solid to go on."

"And how are you going to find that?"

"I don't know. That's my conundrum. I thought you might have some ideas."

"Sorry, my friend," he said. "I'm a little focused on my own survival right now. You want some chocolate pudding? I made it last night and just wasn't hungry."

I didn't want to say no. For all Butch's tough guy act, I knew he was terrified. We all were. It was only when something happened to let you know your terror was justified that the full weight of it overcame you. He was sick, that was obvious. And sick in those days meant the clock was ticking. AIDS was unlike any other disease. It was not an opponent that could be defeated in the ring. It was not cancer. It was not lupus or rheumatoid arthritis. AIDS was the end.

"I'd love some," I lied.

He got up and motioned for me to follow. "This way. Let's sit by the kitchen window and pretend everything is fine."

And that's what we did for the next twenty minutes. We ate pudding and talked about the good times, those few years we had as friends before shadows began to spread over us and the light began to dim. Finally my bowl was empty and it was time to go. He had not touched his.

"I love you," Butch said.

We were standing in his doorway. I was about to leave. Lurline came hurrying in from some hidey hole she kept in the apartment. She eased down onto her haunches at his feet and stared up at me, as if I was the most interesting thing she's seen that day.

"You have to take care of her," he said.

"Pardon me?"

"If anything happens to me. Promise me you'll take care of her, Marshall."

I said yes, of course. Then we kissed and I left him. I was convinced our time together was running short, and that I'd be taking care of that damn cat. Only time would prove me wrong or right, and time was something none of us thought we had.

## TWENTY-FIVE

I REMEMBER LOOKING OVER MY shoulder several times when I left Butch that day. It was as if I feared I might not see him again, a fear based in my own experience. I'd wanted to run back and force him into some kind of treatment—medication, drug trials, a trip to Mexico for a miracle cure with a Yaqui medicine woman—while at the same time knowing it would be futile. No one I knew had survived more than a few months. People didn't win against AIDS; it was like fighting Goliath with no slingshot, no rock, nothing but fury at the certainty of defeat.

All these years later, as a man who's lived long past his expiration date, I know strange things can happen, we can be living anomalies. Maybe that's what made me want to turn around, march back to Butch's front door and shake him into a fighting spirit. But I knew the fight was his alone, as our life and death struggles usually are, so I kept going. Down the elevator, out the front door and onto Gower. I glanced at his building one more time and drove away, not sure if I'd come back or what I'd find if I did: a friend hanging defiantly onto life, or someone else cleaning out his apartment with grief on their face.

I wasn't due on shift at the Parrot for another four hours. My choices of what to do with the time were limited. I could drive home ... and do what? Sit on my couch. Watch for TV news segments on Popper Jack spreading terror in the gay community. See what President Reagan was up to lately—which would not include anything connected to AIDS or the deaths of gay men, subjects he had not found time for in his busy presidential schedule. Another option was lunch. I was hungry by then. The pudding I'd eaten at Butch's place could not be confused with a meal and I was famished. I didn't feel like heading all the way back to the French

Quarter—even then I was forming a plan in my mind and it did not involve backtracking—so I headed to Pedro's Bar & Grill, a Mexican restaurant known for its three alarm tacos and its Tuesday night all-you-can-drink drag shows. I'd keep it light and not too spicy, since I wasn't in the mood to be weighed down.

I got to Pedro's fifteen minutes later. I recognized the valet attendant from the baths—we'd shared a mattress a time or two—and I shrugged when he frowned at me for parking on the street rather than giving the car to him. A dollar was a dollar, and I'd chosen to keep mine in my wallet.

I walked into Pedro's and was immediately greeted with a loud, "Marshall!" by the maître d', a large older woman named Gloria who'd seen me in the place many times with Butch or other friends. She'd added a few unneeded pounds since the last time I'd seen her. Her hair was a different color, too, some unnatural shade of red you'd find in a colorized version of a black and white TV show. She came up to me and threw her bare arms around me.

"Too long, my friend," she said.

"It's been busy," I replied, wriggling out of her embrace.

"Oh, my, all that *stuff* ..."

"Stuff?"

"That killer stuff," she clarified. "At the Parrot, too! Are you okay?"

"I'm fine. And I'm hungry."

"Of course," she said. "Let's put you by the window. Such a pretty day."

She was right. The weather had been spectacular, cool and cloudless. It was the kind of day you might remember the rest of your life, had it not been darkened by death and murder.

On the way to the window table I saw a rack filled with the newest issue of the Blaze. There on the cover was Brad Herring's picture. I reached down and grabbed a copy when we passed.

"You want something to drink?" she said, pulling a chair out for me and handing me a menu she'd grabbed on the way over.

"I'm driving, so no."

"Joey'll be right over for your order. You take care, Marshall, okay?"

"Okay, Gloria," I said.

Joey was taking his sweet time getting to my table on a day when there were only four other people eating there. It was late for lunch and too early for dinner. I spread the Blaze out in front of me and started reading the featured article about their slain reporter.

Brad Herring, it turned out, had gone to Columbia Journalism School in New York City. That alone was impressive, although it begged the question why he would waste such a coveted degree on a rag like the Blaze. Maybe he'd wanted to serve his community, like a doctor going back to his hometown in Appalachia to help his people. The profile was written by the Blaze's editor, a guy named Ed Strong. According to the piece, Herring had grown up in Juniper, Michigan, "a small rural community with one bar, three churches and a mailbox." He'd made his way to Los Angeles after graduating from Columbia and taken an internship at the Blaze that evolved into two years of beat reporting, at which point he was murdered by the subject of his story.

"What can I get you, Mr. Marshall?"

I looked up, startled. Joey had come up to the table without making a sound. He was Latino, younger than me, and as hot as asphalt in July. If his black jeans were any tighter he wouldn't be able to bend over, something I had the feeling Joey was used to doing. He set down a basket of chips and a small bowl of salsa.

"I'll have the beef burrito," I said, "hold the beans and rice."

"Sure thing." He took the menu from the table where I'd laid it and headed off. I dug into the chips and kept reading the article. There wasn't much there. It was mostly a heartfelt, anguished 'in memoriam' for a young man who'd found his calling as a reporter. Everybody at the Blaze loved Brad Herring. He was talented, sweet, a friend's friend, and going places. Blah blah blah. I closed the paper having learned nothing new, formulating my next move while I waited for Joey to struggle back in those pants.

* * *

Half an hour later I was feeling fuller than I'd wanted to be, even without the beans and rice. There were several more people in the restaurant and a second waiter had come on shift. Apparently mid-afternoon was the start of their busy time, especially considering their happy hour kicked in at 2:00 p.m.

I knew what I was going go to do and it involved significant risk. I'd known it before I got to Pedro's, using my time there to convince myself it was the right thing to do and that breaking and entering into someone's apartment, while illegal, was occasionally justified. In this case, three men were dead, killed by a sociopath who may or may not have me in his sights but who had almost certainly interacted with me at the bar.

I was going to visit Phil Seaton's apartment. That was now the plan. I'd been there a couple times back when we'd just met and were having sex. I knew a few pertinent things about the place: it was on the first floor, there were shrubs around most of the building, and Phil had a habit of leaving his bathroom window open. I'd showered in that bathroom. I knew it was in the back of his apartment building, and I knew it was protected by those shrubs. I'd even asked him once if he was worried someone would crawl in through the open window. He'd said he had never thought about it and didn't plan to start. Now that I suspected Phil of involvement in something (I still could not bring myself to think he was Popper Jack; it was too much like admitting your favorite uncle was a pedophile), I was glad he was so nonchalant about the window. Assuming he hadn't changed his ways, I would be able to get into his apartment unseen, look quickly around for anything that might ease or increase my fears, and get the hell out.

Unfortunately, I still had several hours to kill before Phil would be on his way to work. It would be easy enough to call and see if he was out at the time, but that wouldn't tell me anything. He might be running errands or hooking up with some guy he met at Barnsdall Art Park in Hollywood. He'd often talked about cruising there. The only way I could be sure he wasn't coming back was to wait until he was on his way to the Paisley Parrot, and that was another three hours away.

I thought about my options, and finally decided to go see the movie 'Frances' at the Vista movie theater in Silver Lake. I'd been wanting to see it for several weeks, but I knew it was depressing and not something my friends would want to see with me. Given how horrifying real life had become, a downer movie couldn't possibly add to my distress. It also gave me a chance to see the Vista again, a neighborhood icon where gay porn had been shown for years. That's how I knew the place, before they renovated it in 1980 and turned it into a legitimate art house.

Having loosely formulated a plan to commit burglary, I paid my check, waved goodbye to Gloria, gave Joey's ass another quick glance, and headed to my car.

## TWENTY-SIX

I LEFT THE VISTA THEATER with two things in mind. One, my life would never be as difficult as Frances Farmer's in the movie I'd just seen, and two, I was about to commit a crime.

Seeing such a depressing movie only worsened my mood. Fortunately, it had killed three hours of free time and I could now get to the business at hand, which included burglary.

Phil lived on Canyon Drive in one of those low-rise apartment buildings similar to Mac's, only much less fancy. It, too, called itself an estate, but you could tell by the cars in the parking garage that the closest any tenant came to an estate was working on a landscaping crew for $5 an hour.

I parked on Bronson and walked a block, not wanting my car in plain view of the building. I knew Phil would be on his way to work by then. In fact, he'd be expecting me shortly after he got there. But just to be safe, I walked up to the main entrance and rang his buzzer, #1F. I waited, got no response, and rang again. Nowadays I could call him from my cell phone, or even trace his whereabouts with a GPS, but back then life was full of surprises. We didn't know everything with the help of an app at our fingertips and didn't need to. I waited two minutes and decided Phil wasn't home. It was time to put my plan into action.

I headed around to the back of the building. I knew his apartment was a floor-through, with the front facing the street and the back facing a row of tall shrubs. I remembered being in his bathroom at least twice, both times after fevered sex with my favorite bartender. I was a new face at the Parrot in those days and Phil had called dibs on me—at least that's what he told me later. Apparently he wasn't the only one in those dim lights who liked my contours.

I glanced at my watch. It was now 5:30 p.m. and Phil was on his way to the bar, if not already there. I was scheduled to be in at 6:00. I decided I would call him from the phone in his apartment, not a risk before the invention of caller ID, and tell him I was running late on a personal matter. It wasn't a lie.

I glanced both ways to make sure no cars were coming, then gambled that no one was watching the back of the Canyon Drive Estates when a strange man strolled behind the shrubs. I found Phil's apartment three windows down and, sure enough, the window was cracked open several inches. Maybe it was Phil's way of airing out the bathroom, or cutting down the moisture from his showers. Whatever his reasons, it provided a perfect and easy means for me to enter his apartment. I slid the window open, grateful it was wide enough for me to hoist myself up and through it.

The next thing I knew, my body was half in Phil's bathroom and half dangling out the window. I carefully pulled myself through and used the toilet seat to ease myself inside. There was nothing noticeable about it: it was a typical apartment bathroom with a glass shower door. The tile was faux marble and the sink cheap pressboard.

I left the window all the way open in case I had to flee. I stood still on the blue rug he had in front of his sink, listening for any hint of presence in the apartment. Hearing none, I slowly walked into the living room.

Phil's apartment was sparse. He had two posters on the walls, one of Al Pacino in the movie 'Cruising', and one announcing a concert with some new musician named Prince. I'd heard of him but wasn't familiar with his music.

There was a large blond entertainment system on one wall, containing a TV set, stereo, VCR and a CD player. In today's digital world it all seems archaic to me, but at the time these were state of the art. I looked at them a moment, surprised at how well Phil was doing financially to afford these things. I was a bartender, too, and I knew we'd never get rich working at a place like the Paisley Parrot. The biggest tips we got were from customers too drunk to know they'd left a $5 bill on the bar instead of a $1.

There were few photographs in sight, two or three of Phil with people I didn't recognize. One large picture looked to be of Phil and his mother—the one who lived in Phoenix, not Bakersfield.

I don't know what I had expected to find, but I was not finding it. There was no immediate evidence that I was in the apartment of a sadistic serial killer. I skipped the kitchen, pretty sure he would not keep frozen body parts in the refrigerator, and headed instead into his bedroom.

Phil's taste for leather showed in his decorating choices. The bed had a large, dark bedspread on it. When I pulled back a corner I was surprised to see a rubber sheet. That usually meant a free exchange of bodily fluids, water sports, or a rubber fetish. I don't know what I'd expected to find—some harmless, pastel floral print, or just a plain, stained set of yellow sheets. Had my fantasies of domestication with Mac really made me a prude that quickly? I folded the bedspread back the way I'd found it and looked around.

There was a dresser with a large mirror, placed immediately across from the foot of the bed for easy viewing. People like to watch themselves have sex, I've never known why. There were identical nightstands on each side of the bed, one with a dirty ashtray, the other with a lamp. I opened the nightstand drawers, wondering again what I'd expected to find. Evidence that any of the victims had been here?

*Souvenirs, Marshall,* I told myself. *You're looking for souvenirs.* I'd seen enough movies and TV shows to know that serial killers kept mementos. I'd gone to Phil's apartment with the basic assumption he would do the same, and that somewhere in his home I would find a severed finger or Ben Wennig's driver's license. I hadn't been told Ben's license was missing, but it illustrates the point.

I finally made my way to the closet. Phil was not a clothes hound—the guy had three or four pairs of jeans, one blue, the rest black. He had a dozen shirts, four pairs of shoes that I could see, one sport coat, one red windbreaker, and a large metal footlocker.

*A large metal footlocker.* The hair on my arms stood up. I sniffed the air, thinking I might catch a whiff of human decomposition. My mind raced, cluttered with images of what could be in the large box on Phil's closet floor.

I stared down at it. It was black with chrome corner guards, and big enough that it left only a few inches between its front and the closet door. Surprisingly, there was no lock on it.

For some reason I hesitated. I'd gone this far. I had illegally entered a man's apartment. I'd come searching for evidence of murder, and there I stood, looking down at something that could hold what I'd come for, or hold nothing at all.

I could feel myself sweating. I knelt down, flipped up the front latch, and pulled the lid back.

I gasped. There were no souvenirs of killings past, no stash of forget-me-nots taken from dead men.

Half the locker was filled with more cash than I have ever seen in one place, bundled in twenties and tens. The other half was filled with crystal meth—at least that's what I surmised it to be. Large bricks of crystalline white powder wrapped in plastic, with several smaller boxes filled with glassine envelopes of the stuff. Maybe it was cocaine. Maybe it was baby laxative. Whatever it was, it explained everything while explaining nothing.

Phil Seaton was not a killer. He was a drug dealer. We're talking supply-side drugs, the kind of stash that gets people killed or put in prison with a parole hearing in twenty years.

I suddenly wondered about Phil's lax security. The locker wasn't locked. It wasn't a *safe*. There wasn't even a gun resting on top of the cash that he could grab in a pinch. I was sweating through my shirt by then. Something felt off to me, as if a ghost had whispered over my shoulder. I turned around, looked across the bedroom and saw it, up in the corner of the room: a small video camera mounted on the wall near the ceiling. Recording everything. Recording *me.*

*Aw fuck,* I thought. *I'm screwed.*

I thought about climbing up on a chair and yanking the camera out, but what was it connected to? I'd have to toss the apartment looking for a recorder. I knew there wasn't time. I also believed I could play this in a way that might work to my advantage. Phil could be reasoned with, could he not? Or maybe he didn't even check the video. Why would he if he had no reason to suspect anything? *And maybe there is no video footage.* Maybe it's like those 'Beware of Dog' signs people have in their yards when there's no dog inside. It's a preventative measure. A deterrence.

I looked at my watch. I was already late and I hadn't called Phil. At that point I knew I wasn't going to.

I backed my way out along the same path I'd come in. I didn't have time to worry if I'd left any trace. I needed to get to the Parrot and think. Would I say anything to Phil? If so, what would I say, and how would I say it? Or would I just keep my mouth shut and wait to see what happened?

The drive to work that day was the longest I'd ever taken for such a short trip. My thoughts were reeling and conflicted. Phil was my friend. Phil was a criminal. Phil was a trusted confidant. Phil was a liar. Phil had me on tape breaking into his apartment.

The only thing I knew when I walked into the Paisley Parrot that night was that a corner had been turned, and what I saw ahead of me—of us—was a road straight to hell.

## TWENTY-SEVEN

DEREK WAS BEHIND THE BAR when I walked in. I hadn't seen him since he'd filled in for Josef on one of his cocaine hangovers. Derek was reliable—you could count on him to show up in a pinch when someone called in sick, which happened regularly. Come to think of it, Phil had been calling in more often the last few months. I hadn't given it much thought since he never seemed sick when I was around him. I'd figured he might have something, or someone, going on he didn't want me to know about. I'd had no idea that something was dealing meth. We'd minded our own business until I'd crawled through his bathroom window and found a trunk full of money and drugs in his closet.

I'd always liked Derek, even though we seldom interacted, and never outside work. When he was on shift with me he was busy. He was also the quiet type. Short and stocky with a dyed-black crew cut and a small nose ring dangling between his nostrils, Derek gave people the impression he was either slow in the head or a brooding genius. He was definitely good at his job, and he had the added benefit for the Parrot of having his own followers. A dozen or so younger customers would come in when Derek was behind the bar and liven up the place. We knew some of them were there for hustling opportunities and we turned a blind eye. They knew Derek, they knew each other, and they brightened an atmosphere that was too often dreary. It needed it right then; flyers were still pasted around the gayborhood, Popper Jack was still out there, and a pall had settled over most of the bars while everyone waited to read about another murder, or the murderer's capture.

"Where's Phil?" I asked, wondering if he'd called in sick again. If he had, he was definitely not at home. I'd just been there, leaving evidence of my crime on camera—if it was working and not just a deterrent. I doubted the latter. There would be no point in having a non-functioning camera in your bedroom.

"Don't know, man," Derek said, filling a mug with draft for one of his young fans at the bar. "Fat Dick called, told me to come in, that's all I know."

Phil must have called Dick and taken the night off. Calling him directly was unusual but not unheard of, especially since I'd been out all day and couldn't be reached. Dick had all our phone numbers and sometimes called us in for one thing or another, including ad hoc staff meetings when things weren't going to the Bianchis' liking. I expected to have a message from Phil on my answering machine when I got home. Probably one from Dick, too, wondering where the hell I was. I felt a shiver.

"Is he out sick?" I asked, going behind the bar to start my night.

"I don't know. Dick didn't tell me. I didn't ask."

Derek was a man of few words and short sentences.

"Probably going to be slow tonight," I said. "It's been dead since this whole Popper Jack thing."

"That's one way to put it."

He smiled at me and I realized I'd made an inadvertent pun. "It's been *slow*," I amended. "You know what I mean."

"Yeah, I know. If it stays like that tonight, feel free to go home."

"Really?"

He shrugged. "I can use the extra tips. And besides, you got a lot going on from what I hear."

I stared at him. "What have you heard, Derek?"

"Nothing, man. Just … you know … these guys were friends of yours. The dead guys."

"They were not my friends. I dated Ben Wennig, that's true, but I only knew Freddy from the bar and I talked to the reporter Brad Herring exactly once. I didn't know them beyond that. Where did you hear this?"

He shrugged again, an annoying, repetitive gesture he had. At that moment I was leaning toward his being slow in the head rather than a genius.

"Heard it around, you know."

I didn't know and I didn't want to continue the conversation with him. I headed down the bar to see if I could refill any of the four customers we had, then decided to take him up on the offer to go home early if business didn't pick up. I'd be out of there in a few hours and have a rare evening to myself.

Wondering what to do with an unexpected night off, I glanced at the pager on my belt and had an idea.

"Kahlúa and cream," I said, nodding to a man named Lucky sitting at the last stool. I knew he'd been there since noon, when he always showed up. Maybe he was retired; maybe he was just independently wealthy. I had no idea how he supported himself with no obvious job, but I knew what he drank and he appreciated it. That's what makes a place like the Parrot work.

I set about fixing his drink and wondering if Mac could get away for a quick bite. I was going to find out.

## TWENTY-EIGHT

I'D NEVER HAD SEX IN a diner bathroom before but it was fantastic. Just me and Mac squeezed into a men's room the size of a closet. There wasn't even a urinal, just a toilet, a sink, and a mirror I watched his face in while I stood behind him. Our pants were down to our ankles, our smiles reflected back at us in the glass. It was fevered and hurried, over by the time someone began twisting the locked door knob, but so playful and ecstatic I remember it to this day.

To my surprise earlier that evening, Mac responded to my MISSU page, first by knowing what I meant when I punched in 64778, then by calling me at the Parrot.

"Phone's for you," Derek said. I was about to leave, taking him up on his offer for a night to myself. I'd paged Mac an hour earlier and hadn't expected a response at that point.

"Hello?" I said into the receiver. I thought it might be Butch calling to say he'd seen a doctor, or maybe even Phil calling to say where he was.

"Meet me at the Buffalo."

It was Mac, telling me to meet him at the Buffalo Diner on Sunset. Like the French Market, the Buffalo was a popular restaurant frequented heavily by gay people. You could get a short stack on the menu or a quickie in the parking lot, depending on the night. No one knew why it was called the Buffalo, but the name worked and made for easy shorthand. 'Meet me at the Buffalo' was a common phrase in Hollywood.

I didn't ask if he was working. I was just thrilled he was making time to see me in person. Had things turned a corner for us? Had the *investigation* turned a corner?

"I can be there in ten minutes," I said.

"Make it fifteen, I don't want you speeding."

The only thing speeding at that moment was my heart. Without another word, I hung up and told Derek I was leaving. Now. He didn't have a chance to respond before I was out the door and in my car.

* * *

I don't remember how we ended up in the bathroom together—if we got a table first or if he'd just taken my hand and dragged me into the men's room. I remember the door rattling once, then again with someone outside growling, "Enough already, get a room." Apparently we'd been seen going in together. Luckily for them it didn't take long.

"Been awhile?" I asked, smiling as we squeezed by the man who was waiting in the narrow hallway outside. Mac had orgasmed so quickly I guessed it had been several days since his last one.

"Never mind that," he said. Taking my hand, he led me to an empty table and waved at a waiter for two menus.

Ten minutes later he was eating a Reuben sandwich and I was digging into a Cobb salad.

"I thought we weren't supposed to see each other," I said.

"You're worth taking risks for, Marshall James."

He liked saying my full name sometimes, the way other couples might call each other 'Honeybunch' or 'Pumpkin.' I don't know why and I never asked. I just enjoyed it.

"I have something to tell you," I said.

"And I have something to tell *you*."

*Well*, I thought. Here it comes. More rules, more limits. Or was the bathroom sex we'd just had his way of saying goodbye?

"I'll go first," I said, preempting any attempt at telling me something I didn't want to hear. "Phil Seaton is a drug dealer. Maybe out of the Parrot, I don't know, but he's dealing."

He stopped eating. "That's a serious accusation. Where

did you get this information?"

"Let's just say I have it on good authority. An impeccable source."

"Would that source be you?"

The question was direct and disturbing. Did the man I was in love think I was one of Phil's customers? Did he think I used drugs?

"No, it's not me, Mac. I drink, yes, but nothing else. I've seen the damage it does."

"I'm sorry, I had to ask."

"I understand." Knowing we could not get this relationship started on lies of omission, I blurted out the truth. "I got into his apartment and found drugs and money, that's how I know."

He pondered this a moment, then said, "I'll assume you had a key. But what were you doing in his apartment alone? Wait, let me guess. Looking for proof he's the killer."

Unsure what to say, I stayed silent.

"Are you trying to get killed? Jesus, you're a hard case."

"It's too late now," I said. "I saw what I saw. Then I got to the bar and Phil wasn't there. I'm guessing his trip to Bakersfield had something to do with drugs or money, or both. I don't know what's going on with him and I can't ask him until he shows up again."

"You won't ask him at all," Mac said, as firmly as he'd said anything to me. "I have friends in Vice and I'll get this to them. Let them handle it, and stay out of the way. You don't want to get caught up in this."

He was right. I'd been looking for answers to very dangerous questions.

"What were you going to tell me?" I asked.

"Excuse me?"

"Before I spilled the beans about Phil. You had something to tell me."

He slid his plate away, the sandwich half eaten. It was an odd moment of foreboding. He glanced around to make sure no one could hear us, leaned forward and said, "Ben

Wennig wasn't the first."

"I don't understand."

"Popper Jack has been at it for several years."

"How do you know this?"

He sighed. "I'm a cop, remember? I can't say much. I'm already violating my own ethics telling you this, but you're my ... boyfriend, lover, wherever this is going ... and I have to warn you.

"The killer we now call Popper Jack has claimed at least three earlier victims. The poppers are a new touch, but the MO was familiar once we went back and established a pattern. No one connected them until we had a reason to. It pains me to say this, but to a lot of people a gay corpse is just another dead faggot. But you know that."

I knew it all too well. We were dying in increasing numbers and the country had yet to do more than shrug its collective shoulders.

"The earlier killings were spread out over three years. Only one of them even had a missing person's report filed on him."

"So the idea that I'm part of this pattern is just a macabre coincidence?"

He waited a long moment. "I don't know, but he's escalating. He's leaving a calling card now, and I think he knows we're on to him. Maybe he thinks we're closer than we are. If that's the case, he's even more dangerous."

"Maybe it *is* Phil," I said, hearing the panic in my voice. "Maybe he's more than just a dealer and maybe he's crazy from the drugs and maybe ..."

"It's not Phil," he said with troubling certainty.

"And what makes you so sure of that?"

"Because we've looked into it ... into *him*."

"What?" I heard my voice rise and saw people turn toward our table. "So you knew this already? The dealing or whatever he's involved in?"

"Yes and no. We've been looking at everyone connected to the Paisley Parrot. For drugs and hustling. For money laundering. We know who owns the place, Marshall."

I was stunned. Whoever 'we' was, they had been surveilling the bar, maybe coming in undercover. That's what it sounded like to me, and I didn't like it.

"Am I on your radar, too?" I asked.

He didn't answer, and I knew I was officially part of their investigation.

"Am I being watched?" I persisted.

"Not that I know of."

*"Not that you know of?"*

"This investigation isn't just me. I'm only a small part of it, and they know about us, or at least that I've been with you. I can't keep something like that secret, you have to understand that."

"I understand fine," I said, disgusted by the sulk in my voice. I couldn't help it. I didn't know who to believe or trust. I didn't know at that moment if Mac's affection for me was sincere or if I was somehow part of a larger game plan to catch a serial killer.

"Don't you need to get back to work?" I asked. "There must be a dead body behind a motel somewhere."

He knew I was hurt and angry. He reached across the table and placed his hand on mine. I felt my anger fade and wondered if I was a fool to trust him.

"Yes, I do need to get back to work," he said. "But I had to see you."

"You didn't just need quick sex?" I asked, my smile giving me away.

"You're more to me than sex," he replied. Not much in the way of assurance, but somehow enough.

We motioned to the waiter and got separate checks. We walked out into the crisp January air. There, in front of the large plate glass window of the Buffalo Diner, we kissed. I'd expected it to be brief, maybe just a peck on the cheek. Instead, Mac McElroy kissed me with a burning urgency, as if we might never kiss again. Finally he stepped back, said, "I really do love you, Marshall James," and turned away for his car.

"I love you, too," I said.

I remember thinking I'd whispered it, when my impulse was to shout. But I was afraid then. I didn't know what was coming at me, or from which direction. Death? Love? Both?

I watched him get into his unmarked car and drive away, waving at me in his rearview mirror. It was a sight I've never forgotten.

## TWENTY-NINE

I WOKE UP THE NEXT morning wondering where I could escape to while I waited for this deadly storm to pass. Europe and South America weren't possibilities on a bartender's wages. I couldn't make an extended visit to my brother or sister—we hadn't spoken since our father's death. The life I'd led left me with limited options for hiding.

After watching Mac drive off the night before, I'd gone home and mulled everything over until my head was throbbing. I hadn't known you could think yourself into a migraine, but that's what it felt like; between anxiety, dread, and a sense that things were spiraling out of control, I'd developed a headache on the high end of the Richter scale. I'd responded with several aspirin and a brandy nightcap, then laid on the couch with my eyes closed. Emotionally and mentally exhausted, I'd drifted quickly off and slept straight through for nine hours, waking up at 6:00 a.m. convinced I should leave California immediately. Half an hour and two cups of coffee later, I'd dispelled the notion that fleeing was a solution.

Caffeine had the effect of focusing me. Just when I was beginning to think rationally again, the phone rang. The sun wasn't fully up yet. Nobody had called me that early since my father died and they needed someone to make funeral arrangements. I sat up on the edge of the couch and reached for the phone.

"Hello?" I was expecting a wrong number.

"Thank God you're okay! ... *Are* you okay?"

It was Butch's voice. My first reaction was gratitude he was alive and sounding much healthier. I'd worried since I'd seen him he might be one of those who went in a flash, gone so quickly there was no chance to say goodbye. My second reaction was worry.

"What are you talking about, Butch?" I asked.

"It was on the six o'clock news."

"What, for godsake? Another body?"

"Yes and no."

By then I was getting annoyed. I reached for my cigarettes and pulled one out, lighting it with a Zippo one of the Parrot regulars gave me for Christmas.

"Please make some sense," I said, blowing a cloud of smoke into the room.

"It's Phil."

I felt the hair on the back of my neck rise.

"What about Phil?"

"They found his body in Griffith Park."

"Aw, Jesus. Popper Jack, I'm assuming."

There was a moment's hesitation. "I don't think so with this one. That's why I called you. The TV reporter said it appears he was shot execution style."

*Money. Drugs. Shot execution style.* It was an equation that shouldn't have shocked me, but it did.

"That's it?" I asked. "Were there any more details?"

"A jogger found his body off one of the running paths when he went into the bushes to piss."

"They said that on TV?"

"No, silly, they said 'relieve himself' or something like that. What difference does it make? The body wasn't in an obvious place, but whoever killed him didn't make much effort to hide it. Like it was a message."

"Well it wasn't a message to me, Butch!" I said, hearing anger in my own voice.

"I didn't say it was. Why would you think that?"

*Let's see, I broke into his apartment yesterday, possibly when he was being shot in the head somewhere else. I found a trunk of drugs and money in the closet, and by the way, I was caught on camera … but no, I don't know anything about it.*

"Can I call you back?" I said. "I feel a headache returning."

"Returning?"

"It's a long story. Did you get to a doctor?"

"I did, Marshall. And we'll talk later."

All my life I've hated being told by anyone we would 'talk later.' I didn't like it with Butch, I hated it with my father, and I don't like it with Boo. It has the sound of a doctor waiting to give you a cancer diagnosis in person.

"Just tell me one thing now," I said. "Are you going to die on me soon or not?"

"I'll do my best not to," he said. "And I'm sorry if I started your morning off poorly."

"Poorly is an understatement. But on the upside, I had sex with Mac last night in the bathroom of the Buffalo Diner."

"Really! Details, please."

I waited a moment for effect, then said, "We'll talk later."

"Fuck you," he said, laughing.

We hung up and I returned to my coffee and cigarettes. I was not going to turn on the television. Phil was dead. Trying to find out more about it on the local news would not give me answers or improve my chances of survival.

# THIRTY

THE DAY DRAGGED ON, MINUTE by minute like a slow motion car accident. Everything had felt that way, from the arrival of Popper Jack to falling in love with a cop. As if I was driving past the wreckage of my own life and craning to see if anyone was hurt, where the blood was coming from and if the man in the driver's seat was me.

I was panicked that the police would find my fingerprints in Phil's apartment—I hadn't made any attempt to wipe them since I never expected him to be dead. I knew they'd find them when they dusted the place. I'd been arrested once for solicitation in my early Hollywood days. My prints were on file. It was only a matter of time, probably days, before they came looking for me.

And that made me wonder again: if they'd been watching Phil, as Mac had said—if they knew he was dealing—were they watching me, too? We worked together at the Parrot. They might make assumptions. Had they seen me crawl into his bathroom window? And then I had a darker thought: if they'd been watching Phil and me, or Phil and the bar, was it possible they'd seen Popper Jack selecting his prey? Had they let him commit murder rather than tip Phil off to their surveillance?

*That's insane, Marshall,* I thought. There was simply no logical reason the police would let a killer indulge his depravity so they could catch a drug dealer. What was possible, however, was that somewhere in their watching, in their photographs and recordings or whatever they used to keep tabs on a suspect, they had an image of the real Popper Jack. I made a note to talk to Mac about it, then headed to the Parrot for the night.

Overwhelmed by it all, I was deep into a fog of confusion when I finally got to work. I'd walked there looking over my shoulder every few steps. It felt like an involuntary twitch, turning my head slightly and straining my peripheral vision, listening for the sound of footsteps behind me. I'd felt followed every since Mac told me the cops were on to Phil and the Bianchis. And there was that whole business of the camera in Phil's apartment. I couldn't help feeling observed—but by whom?

I walked through the front curtain and saw Derek behind the bar again. He looked unhappy, as if breathing was a burden and being at work was as much as he could bear. *Grim* would describe the expression on his face.

"What's up?" I asked, immediately feeling stupid. What *wasn't* up? At least six men were dead at the hands of a psychopath, if what Mac had told me was true and this was the same guy. Phil was killed by somebody unhappy with his side job as drug dealer and possible thief—all that cash could have been stolen—and I was probably on the verge of being accused of involvement with it all.

Derek didn't say anything. He just looked toward the office door and tilted his head slightly.

"Fat Dick?" I said, understanding now why he was in such a foul and anxious mood.

He nodded, then said, "And he wants to see you."

I wasn't especially afraid of Dick. Staff at the Parrot had very little direct contact with him. He was a arge, unpleasant presence who came in every Wednesday, spent a few hours in the back office, and left with a significant amount of cash somewhere on his person. *Where* he put the money had always been a mystery to me, and one I didn't think too much about: wondering where a trusted mob underling concealed several thousand dollars in small bills was the kind of curiosity that got your legs broken.

And while I wasn't overly intimidated by him, I had no desire to be in a small confined space with the man. However, I knew refusal was not an option. When Dick wanted to meet you with, it wasn't a request. I took a deep breath, fidgeted with a stack of napkins on the bar to buy myself another few seconds, then headed back to the office. On the count of three, I knocked.

Richard Montagano wasn't so much fat as he was big. The guy was close to six feet, and large in a way that suggested unusually big bones covered by one part fat and two parts muscle. They could have called him Big Dick instead, which would have sounded even more ridiculous and thrilled him to no end.

He was sitting behind a desk in a black leather chair that had arm rests and a high back. The leather was torn from wear and looked almost shredded. He was several times too large for the chair and I wondered why it hadn't collapsed under him long ago.

"Have a seat," he said, his attention on some papers spread out in front of him and a calculator he was punching with a ball point pen. He did not look up at me. He did not call me 'Marshall,' he did not call me 'James.' He did not call me anything.

"Mr. Montagano ..." I said, hoping to get the conversation moving and over.

"Shut up, I'm working."

I wondered why he would want me in the office if he was working and expected me not to speak.

I sat in silence a full two minutes, when finally he pushed a button on the calculator, took the long strip of paper it spat out and ripped it from the machine. He stuck the strip under an ashtray and looked up at me at last.

"You know why you're here?" he asked.

I was struck by his eyes, which I'd never looked into before, any more than I would look into the eyes of a growling pit bull. They were dark brown pools, and he had unusually long lashes I could see even in an office lit only by a desk lamp.

"What are you looking at, James?"

He'd said my name. He'd also made me acutely aware I was staring at him, a risky thing to do with Fat Dick.

"Nothing, Mr. Montagano. And no, I don't know why

I'm here."

"We're short staffed," he said.

I could swear he winked very slightly when he said it. I assumed he was talking about Phil, but calling it 'short staffed' when a man had been shot in the head seemed a little detached to me.

"If you mean Phil …"

"I mean we're down a bartender and he ain't coming back."

I knew in that moment who had killed Phil Seaton. Did they know I knew what Phil was up to? Did they know I'd seen the drugs and money?

"I might know someone who'd be interested …"

"We don't want anybody else, kid. We want you."

I felt my stomach turning over.

"Mr. Montagano …"

"Call me Dick," he said, offering the kind of smile that leaves a blood trail. "You do anyway, right? You and the others. 'Fat Dick' I think it is."

"I wouldn't know about that …"

"Don't fucking lie to me!" he shouted.

I imagined Derek listening outside the door and hurrying away at the sound of yelling.

"Don't ever lie to me." More calmly then, in charge. "And don't take this as an offer. It's an order. We need someone to take over for Phil, God rest his soul."

"What exactly is the job description?" I asked weakly.

"I'll let you know. I just wanted to give you a heads up—you'll be running the night shift here, maybe do some other things the family needs done, so keep it on the up and up, we're watching."

It was the first time I was aware of that Fat Dick had ever mentioned the 'family.' We all knew he answered to the Bianchis, but the name was not to be spoken out loud. Nothing was ever to be said about the mob, the mafia, or organized crime. The Paisley Parrot was a legitimate business, just ask Oscar LeGrand, wherever he was buried.

I waited in silence, full of questions but not daring to ask any of them.

"Why are you still here?" he said.

I started to get out of my chair. Possessed by a need to say something, anything, I blurted out, "I think Popper Jack is somebody who comes here. Maybe somebody who's been coming here a long time."

It wasn't what he'd expected to hear from me. He sat back in his chair, staring at me a long moment as if I were a bug under a glass.

"Is this an informed guess, or you just have a feeling?"

"The victims, at least the last three—"

"The last three?"

"There were more. I can't say how I know, but I know. Maybe they drank at the Parrot, too. The last three did for sure, and it got me thinking this might be where he finds his targets."

"Like, scopes them out and whatnot?"

For a moment he seemed interested. Then he said, "Thanks for the tip, kid. We're on it."

So it was true—the Bianchis had put a hit out on a serial killer. It was all too much for me and I wanted out of the small, suffocating room with him.

"Right, you're on it, of course." I got up to leave. "I appreciate the job offer, Dick …"

"I told you it's not an offer." He smiled at me again and I felt my blood go cold. "It's a promotion."

I didn't bother thanking him again. There was no point in it, and nothing to be thankful for.

I left the office and closed the door behind me.

"So?" asked Derek, leaning against the bar.

I ignored him, walked to the liquor shelf and grabbed a bottle of Jack Daniels.

# THIRTY-ONE

THE REST OF THE NIGHT was a slow descent into a brownout. For the uninitiated, a brownout is the weak sister of a blackout, less frightening but still a symptom of a drinking problem on the rise. It's one of those drunken episodes you sort of remember the next day, a void of lost memory lit by stars of recollection: *Oh, yeah, I remember saying that*, and, *Christ, did I really do that? I must have, because I remember parts of it*. Blackouts—a full-on loss of time and everything you did during it—may be more merciful. At least then you can pretend the worst of what your friends say you did must be exaggerated.

I'm making it sound worse than it was. After all, I was at work. I didn't throw up on into a customer's martini, I didn't strip and invite anyone to do with me as they pleased. Derek covered me as best he could. He began taking most of the orders so I wouldn't risk slurring my words when I talked to the dozen people at the bar. And the traffic was still light as people stayed away, waiting for an arrest in the Popper Jack case. No one wanted to be the next body found.

Finally Derek told me to just go home. It was nearing midnight and our patrons had dwindled to six or seven diehards—the drunks who would still be sitting there even if they died, their corpses propped up with their heads on the bar. I said thanks as coherently as I could and was about to leave when Mac walked in.

This is where the brownout got a little lighter, with a degree of sobriety returning as I forced my mind into a semi-conscious state.

"Mac?" I said, as startled as I was happy to see him. I was about to lift the divider that gave us access to the work area.

"Hey, Marshall James," he said, walking up to me, using

my full name again, making me melt in my mild stupor.

I was grateful for the bar between us. I wanted to throw my arms around him, but I knew I was too loaded and I probably smelled it. I hoped the stale bar air and the cigarette smoke masked my own boozy odor.

"What …?" I managed.

"We need to talk."

"I'm just getting off."

"Looks like you've been getting off for awhile."

I let the comment slide. "Did you want to go somewhere?"

He glanced at his watch. "You're finished this early?"

I nodded toward Derek. "It's okay, he's got it covered and we're slow tonight. Every night, actually. The whole Popper Jack business."

I knew I'd sounded dismissive—*the whole Popper Jack business*—as if a brutal serial killer and multiple victims were nothing major.

"You know what I mean," I said quickly.

He nodded and I wasn't sure if he was agreeing with me or just moving the conversation along. "Let's to go my car," he said.

I didn't question him, although talking in his car was a new situation. I came out from behind the bar, waved at Derek to let him know I was leaving, and headed outside with Mac.

I'd seen Mac's vehicle several times, beginning at the crime scene when I'd discovered Ben's body, but I'd never been in it. It was a standard issue unmarked car, a black Ford. I didn't know the model—cars were never my thing—but I knew the type. Everybody who'd spent more than ten minutes on the streets knew an unmarked cop car, just like we could spot a cop out of uniform from across a crowded room.

Mac got into the driver's seat, then reached over and opened the passenger door for me.

I was feeling much more clear headed by then. I

wouldn't call it sober. Nobody with six or seven stiff drinks in them is sober, but I no longer felt like I was sliding into oblivion.

What I noticed immediately was that the car didn't smell like smoke. Mac wasn't a smoker, unlike a lot of other cops and plenty of civilians at the time. I was used to the stale smell of cigarettes in bars, restaurants and automobiles. Mac's car didn't smell like an ashtray.

"It's so good to see you. Are you on duty?" I said, having closed the car door.

I remember reaching my hand over and putting it on his thigh. It may have been inappropriate in a cop car, but he didn't stop me. He let my palm rest there a moment. Then, surprisingly, he took my hand and put it back in my own lap.

"Not now," he said. "I am on duty. I'm also not supposed to be seeing you—diner bathrooms notwithstanding. But this is very serious, Marshall."

He left off the 'James.' This was serious indeed. I waited for him to continue.

He turned to me and said, "The Phil Seaton case is not mine, but we all work in the same unit, the same room as a matter of fact. We share information. And what I know is that they found the trunk in Seaton's closet."

"Good!" I said.

He put up his hand to stop me. "Hold on, Marshall. 'Good' is not what I'd call it. There was no cash in the trunk, no drugs."

"But I saw it, Mac. It was there."

"I don't doubt you, bud ..."

"'Bud?'" I said, a little too drunkenly. "I'm not 'Marshall James' anymore? Or your boyfriend? I'm 'Bud?'"

He looked at me quizzically. "Are you drunker than I thought?"

The statement made me burn with shame. I forced it down, tried to shrug it off. "Just a little," I said.

"Any is too much, Marshall. It's not a good look for you.

And 'bud' is just an expression. It doesn't mean anything. What matters is that they didn't find anything in the trunk in a dead man's apartment but they did find your fingerprints."

I stared at him, afraid to say anything.

"Solicitation? Really?"

I felt my face get hot again. "Yes, Mac, I turned a few tricks when I first moved to Hollywood. You'd be surprised at what people do to survive."

"I wouldn't be surprised at all. And I don't judge you for it. I don't *care* what you did in the past. We've all done things we regret. But let's stay on point here. They knew you were in Phil's apartment. They know there *were* drugs in the trunk because they tested it. You can take ten pounds of crystal out of a trunk but you can't take the residue, not without running the whole thing through a car wash."

"Did they find anything else?"

He turned and stared at me, making me wait for effect. "You mean, like a camera?"

There was no point in lying. He obviously knew there was a camera in Phil's bedroom. "That would be what I'm referring to."

"There was no film in it."

So I'd been right! There was no film in the camera.

"The tape was gone," he added. "That doesn't mean it was never there."

I didn't know what to make of it. If there had been videotape, where did it go? To the same place the cash and drugs went? I couldn't sort it out then, I was still intoxicated and increasingly frightened.

"So they know I was telling the truth," I said, changing the direction.

"They know something went on. They know Phil Seaton was dealing, which they'd already suspected. But they don't know for whom, or how far up the chain it goes."

"Up the chain?"

"To a drug lord. Or, they think more likely, to the

Bianchis."

It only confirmed why Fat Dick had been unconcerned with Phil's death: because he knew about it ahead of time.

"You think he was dealing for them?" I said, as sober by that point as I would be until I'd slept it off.

"I think he was either dealing for them and skimming off the top—which would explain the cash—or he was working independently in contradiction to their interests. That's what we think."

"We?"

"Homicide and Vice," he said. "It's a joint operation now."

"What about Popper Jack? What about Ben and Freddy and Brad Herring? Are they just collateral damage in something bigger?"

"Nothing's bigger than a serial killer," he assured me. "But we can walk and chew gum at the same time."

"Of course you can," I said, reaching my hand back and resting it on his leg, less suggestively this time.

"I have something to ask you," he said.

"You're proposing to me in a cop car?"

"You're being stupid now. It's not a marriage proposal. Maybe someday, if we can ever get married … but no, it's much more serious than that at the moment."

I waited, not knowing what to expect. If he wasn't going to ask me to spend my life with him, or leave my job and run away to an island, what did he want? The suspense mounted. I couldn't imagine what this man, this *cop* I was more in love with by the hour, was going to ask me.

"We need you to wear a wire," he said.

I remember blinking. I remember not being able to process the request. I knew what 'wearing a wire' meant, but I was so unprepared for it that I just stared at him.

"Are you okay?" he said finally.

"Yes, sure," I replied. "I just … don't think I understand."

"It's a complicated situation with a simple explanation.

You work at the Parrot, you have access to Richard Montagano ..."

"Fat Dick."

"Yes, Fat Dick—I won't ask how he got that name."

"It's more muscle than fat," I said.

"Whatever it is, he's a lieutenant for the Bianchis and if they killed Phil Seaton, he knows it."

"Now that you mention it," I said, "Dick just had a conversation with me earlier this evening. He wants me to take Phil's job. It's a promotion, if that's what you call getting closer to the mouth of a snake."

His eyes widened. "This is perfect," he said. "If you're willing to do this ..."

"What's expected of me?" I said. I felt my stomach churn and my bowels loosen slightly.

Mac proceeded to tell me what they wanted me to do.

When he was finished explaining it to me, after I'd nodded 'Yes,' we sat in silence for several minutes. A line had been crossed—several, in fact. Finally, he took my hand and lifted it to his lips. He kissed my fingers.

"What if I get killed?" It was as blunt, and as necessary, as I could be.

"Don't think that. You will not get killed. I won't let that happen."

"You, personally?"

"Me, personally," he said. He opened his jacket and showed me his service pistol in a shoulder holster. "*Me. Personally.*"

He pulled me to him—it was too awkward for him to slide over with the steering wheel in the way—and kissed me hard, right there in his patrol car. I knew it was real. But I wasn't convinced, not really, that I wouldn't end up dead. People like the Bianchis didn't care about promises made between men in love, even if one was a cop.

"Let me take you home," he said.

"I'd rather walk. I need to think, and sober up a little more."

"A lot more. You smell like a bottle of whiskey."

We kissed again quickly, then I let myself out of the car and started walking up the street. I knew he was watching me, waiting for me to turn a corner before he drove back into the night.

# THIRTY-TWO

ITHE NEXT MORNING I FOUND myself in the same interview room I'd been in when Mac first slid his hand across the table and placed it on mine. That moment seemed like the distant past to me, when in fact it had only been two weeks. Since then three more people had died, I'd been told by the mob to take over for one of their flunkies, and now I was being asked by the FBI to help them bring down the Bianchi crime family.

The room felt much smaller with six people in it. Mac stood against a wall, his arms folded, glancing at me without locking eyes. I didn't know how much his colleagues knew about us. They knew I was a witness after the fact to the Ben Wennig murder, if that's what you call someone who finds a corpse. They knew Mac had asked me to help them nail the Bianchis through Fat Dick. And now, seeing me rip my fingernails and shake my leg like a speed freak, they knew I was scared shitless.

The other people in the room included two detectives, maybe Homicide, maybe Vice, nobody said. Both were in their forties from the looks of it, one a guy named Dean Randall, the other a woman named Rita Crescent. Dean was in a chair opposite me, while Rita stood next to Mac along the wall.

The final two were more mysterious and more intimidating: the Feds. Both were men, and humorless from what I could tell. They'd dispensed with any good-cop-bad-cop routine, if they'd ever had one. Todd Stanton was one, Jim Barnes the other. I knew because Mac introduced them when I first arrived. Crew cuts, suits, guns in shoulder holsters under their jackets. Heavies.

I'd been in the room with them all for twenty minutes while they explained the gravity of what they were doing and what they were asking me to participate in. Without giving me too much information (I was a civilian, after all), they explained they'd been working the Bianchi case for the past two years and finally had a chance to strike at the heart of the family—with my assistance. I was the rare opportunity for them to get as close to Anthony Bianchi as they'd ever gotten. They confirmed their suspicion he'd had his father Gregory killed, but they'd have to prove it without a body, if they ever could. Gregory Bianchi, like Oscar LeGrand, had vanished from the earth.

"Kevin tells us you've been asked by Richard Montagano to take over work duties for the late Phil Seaton."

It was Todd speaking. Under different circumstances I'd say he was attractive, in a paramilitary way. "You mean Fat Dick," I said.

"Yes," Todd replied. "That would be Richard Montagano. Although I'm told people who call him Fat Dick don't always live to regret it."

He smiled, breaking the ice as much as it was going to be broken.

"So let me get this straight," I said. "You want me to have a conversation with Fat Dick and get him to admit to killing Phil."

"That's not likely," said Jim, the other FBI agent. He looked the way he spoke—short, thick, and to the point.

"Why?" I asked. "Because he thinks I might be recording him?"

"No, Mr. James. If he thought that, you'd be dead in minutes, maybe seconds."

"He'd shoot me while it was being recorded?"

"He'd probably strangle you with one hand while he yanked out the wire with the other." It was Todd again, practicing his gallows humor. It wasn't working.

Jim continued: "Montagano won't admit to anyone outside the Bianchis' inner circle that he was involved in a murder, or that they were. But it's very possible he will finally reveal some … let's call it highly confidential information … to you, just as he must have with Phil Seaton."

"You think Phil was working for the Bianchis?"

They looked at each other, then Todd said, "Whoever he was working for was pissed off enough to put a bullet in his head and dump his body in Griffith Park. And if he was working for himself, he'd gone rogue and they weren't happy about it."

"The Bianchis are the last of a breed in L.A." It was Mac, speaking from his place along the wall. "The West Coast is different. The Mafia still holds power in New York and Chicago, but out here they've been all but shut down, even in Vegas."

"Especially in Vegas," added the lady cop, Rita.

"When we bring the Bianchis down, that's the end of it," Mac continued. "They'll pop back up here and there, roaches always do, but they'll be finished as a force. You'd be helping close a long, ugly chapter in L.A.'s history. Think about that."

"I have," I said. "I'll do this. For my country, I guess, and because it's the right thing. And because …" I looked at Mac. He knew what I was thinking. *And because Mac asked me to.* I couldn't say that, not to strangers in a conference room asking me to gamble with my life. Instead, I said, "… because I can. But will it be the last thing I ever do?"

I saw a stricken look flash across Mac's face: he would not allow me to be put in harm's way, or at least not close enough for it to kill me. I believed that to be true, but not with the rest of them.

"We'll be right outside in a van, listening to every word," said the Fed named Jim. "We'll be ready to intervene at the slightest sign of danger to you."

"Being in the same room alone with Fat Dick is dangerous enough," I said. "I'm trusting you with my life, that much is obvious. I doubt Dick would kill me right there in the Parrot, but I probably wouldn't get two blocks outside it before some black sedan pulled up and told me to get in."

"We know that," Todd said. "We'll be right there. Nothing will happen to you, Mr. James."

"Will you arrest him if … *when* he says something incriminating?"

They looked at each other and I could tell they were keeping something from me.

"It's part of a bigger picture," Jim said, too carefully.

"So the answer is no. You just want him on record saying something you can use later."

"That's how these investigations work." This time it was the detective named Dean, who hadn't spoken since saying hello when I first walked in. "Rita and I work with Mac in the Homicide Division. We're investigating the murder of Phil Seaton, as well as the Popper Jack killings."

"You think they're connected?"

"We're not in the business of speculating."

What he said was absurd on its face. Investigators were very much in the business of speculating. But there was no possible connection I could see between Phil's execution, the Bianchi crime family, and a serial killer I now knew had been perfecting his game for several years.

Dean continued, "Agents Stanton and Barnes are investigating the Bianchis. If Dick Montagano admits to killing Seaton, as unlikely as that is, he'll be arrested very quickly. It's much more possible that he'll pull the curtain back just a little on the Bianchis' operations as a way to bring you in, and what you see there—"

"You mean what I *hear* there," I said.

"Precisely. What you hear there is what we'll use to bring them down."

"We're just making the point that the cases are separate but connected," said Mac, using his professional voice.

"Symbiotic, you might say," added Rita.

"*Symbiotic*, right," I said. "Well, now what? What if Fat Dick doesn't call me in for another little tete-a-tete for a week or two?"

The FBI guys looked at each other again. Did they think I didn't see them? I was sitting three feet away.

"We want you to make contact," Todd said.

"Give Montagano a call," said Jim. "Tell him you're interested in his offer and you'd like to talk in the office."

Todd again: "Ask him what kind of advancement opportunities there are."

"So basically tell him I'm looking for information that could put him in prison for the rest of his life?" I said.

"He won't think that if you do this right," said Todd, unable to hide the irritation in his voice.

"Fine," I said. "I'll make the call. I'll wear the wire. But not today. Today I want to leave here, act like my life's not in imminent danger, and enjoy myself. May I do that?"

"Certainly, Mr. James," said Mac.

*Great,* I thought. *Now it was 'Mr. James.'* From a man I'd had sex with in a diner bathroom. Everything felt more like a bad dream I couldn't shake off, when I finally got up from the conference table and said my goodbyes.

"We'll be in touch," Todd Stanton, FBI agent, giant slayer, said to me with a quick, dry handshake. "But just in case you need to call …" He handed me his business card, which I slipped into my shirt pocket.

I started to ask if they knew how to reach me, then realized of course they did. They're the FBI.

They all filed out of the room except Mac. Putting his hand on my arm he said, "I'll show you out, Marshall James."

I jerked my arm away. "It was 'Mr. James' two minutes ago."

"We'll talk," he said.

"About *what*? Do you want to go forward with this relationship or not, *Mr.* McElroy? Or should I say 'Detective.' Is that what this is about? You have to keep them separate? I don't know if I can live with that."

"We'll talk about everything, but obviously not here."

"Obviously. And thanks anyway, but I can show myself

out."

I left him there, stung but not surprised. What I'd said was true: I didn't know if I could involve myself with a man who led two distinct lives. It wasn't that one was a lie—neither of Mac's lives was false—but that his job demanded he keep a wall between them, *between us*.

I left the police station shaken, worried and unsure. I needed comfort, the presence of someone whose voice had always been as reliably calming as a sedative.

I pulled a quarter out of my pocket and headed for a payphone.

## THIRTY-THREE

"THANK YOU FOR NOT ASKING me to meet you at Creep Stanley's," I said.

Butch had taken pity on me when I'd called, agreeing to meet at the Buffalo Diner. It was a longer drive for him but the worry in my voice had convinced him to travel.

We were sitting in a booth with a view of the men's room.

"What are you looking at?" he asked, seeing me glance at the bathroom door a third time, or maybe it was the fourth.

"Honestly? We had sex in that bathroom a few nights ago."

He stared at me, uncomprehending, but not about having sex in a restaurant toilet. It wasn't that unusual. "Who is 'we'?" he finally said.

"Me and Mac."

"Ah, of course. The guy you're sizing rings with."

"Cock rings, maybe," I said, and laughed for the first time in at least two days. "But yes, it's serious. I just wouldn't pick out a best man's tuxedo yet if I were you."

"The operative word being 'yet.'"

I smiled. Butch was looking rested. This was a rare and beautiful thing. I dared to hope Butch was one of 'them'—the guys who stumped science and ended up in studies, the ones with genetic mutations and the kind of luck that wins lotteries. It was too early then to call anyone a longtime survivor; as far as we knew, HIV had only been around a couple years. But there were a few who kept living and gave the rest of us reason to believe we might get old.

"You make it to the doctor yet?" I asked.

"Yeah," he said, looking down at a Reuben sandwich he'd barely touched. "I've got it, Marshall, that's a fact. But I have improved and the doctor's cautiously optimistic.

I could tell by his fidgeting he didn't want to talk more about it.

"So what's going on?" he said. "You sounded scared. Fear is not something I associate with you."

He was right. I wasn't scared being a gay kid in Indiana, once I beat the crap out of a couple kids who thought I was an easy target. I wasn't scared moving to Hollywood and working the streets when I had to. I wasn't even scared of the virus. We didn't know enough yet to have safe sex, or what that meant. But I'd used rubbers since high school to avoid any diseases. I also figured a time comes for all of. You do the best you can and leave the rest to the capricious nature of life and God—if you believe in one.

"I'm in over my head," I said, raising my hand as far up as I could stretch. "So far over I'm afraid I'm going to drown, Butch."

"Is this about Phil?"

"Phil. Mac. Fat Dick. And Popper Jack. We can't forget about Popper Jack."

"What's your part in it? You wouldn't be freaked out if there wasn't one."

"*Everything*, that's my part in it. I'm in love with Mac. I've been asked by Fat Dick to take over for Phil at the Parrot. And Popper Jack's killing people I know ... or *was* killing them. He's hasn't struck since Brad Herring, the reporter."

"Maybe he left town. Good news, bad news, you know? We catch a break while some other community gets terrorized."

"I don't know what to think about any of it," I said. "But they've asked me to wear a wire and try to get Fat Dick on tape admitting to something."

"Something?"

"Involving Phil's murder, or the Bianchis running the Parrot, Red River, whatever else they've got going on in this city."

"Don't the cops know what the Bianchis are up to?"

I gobbled up the last of my french fries. Unlike Butch, I'd been starving. "It's not just the LAPD. It's the FBI, too. And of course they know. But they have to prove it. They're out to bring down the whole operation and they need something ironclad."

"Like a confession to murder…"

I could hear the skepticism in his voice. "Leverage," I explained. "Something to hold over him. He won't confess to murder. But he might implicate himself or the Bianchis in some way. That's where I come in."

"What if you get killed?"

It was an obvious question, one I'd asked myself a dozen times since my meeting at the police station that morning.

"Mac assured me …"

"Is Mac going to be in the room with you?"

"Well—"

"Is Mac going to be within firing distance, in case Fat Dick figures out you're recording him and tries something?"

"It's not—"

"I'd say no if I were you, Marshall."

This wasn't the response I'd hoped for from Butch. I wanted to be reassured, not doubted.

"I can't go back on this. I told them I'd to it."

He slid his plate away, leaned toward me over the table and said, "Listen to me. Life is very, very short. Mine may be shorter than most, we don't know yet. But I can tell you that I will not spend one more day doing what I don't want to do, believing things I don't really believe, or making commitments I have no desire to keep. I quit my job, Marshall."

I sat back, not sure I'd heard him correctly. "You took time off?"

"No, I quit. It's over. I don't want to be a paralegal. I hate the legal profession. I can't stand wearing a tie to work, and I don't have time for corporate bullshit. I called in sick one day last week, and walked away the next. I haven't been back and I won't be. I'm a free man."

"Without a job."

Wrong thing to say, wrong time. Butch pulled back. I could see from the anger in his eyes that he had not expected me to question his decision, any more than I'd thought he would question mine.

"Truce," I said. "You know I love you. I support you completely. And I need you to support me. You just said yourself life's a crap shoot, in so many words. You might be the one to beat this thing—I hope you are—and I might be the one to bring down the Bianchis and live to tell about it. So let's leave it there. I've got your back, you've got mine."

He cocked his head slightly and looked at me, a wistful smile creeping across his lips. "We do indeed, Marshall. I remember that kid—you were a kid to me then, maybe you always will be—hustling for money to get a room at the Spa."

"Long time ago."

"And just yesterday, like all of life. It flies, my friend. Don't hurry it with a dangerous game."

"It's not a game, Butch. I trust the cops. I trust the FBI. I trust Mac. The rest is going to have to play itself out."

"So when is this big wiretapping going down?"

"I don't know yet," I said, waving at our waiter for the check. "I have to set it up with Dick. I don't even know what a wire looks like. Does it hurt?"

"You're going to find out," he said, pulling out his wallet.

"I've got this," I said, waving away his money. "You can take me out to lunch a year from now. I expect you to still be around."

"I'm trying, Marshall, I really am."

I knew he was, and I knew he would probably be dead within a year, but sometimes pretending is the only way to keep going.

I handed the waiter a credit card and slid out of the booth.

"I'll be back in a minute," I said. "I just want to—"

"Check out the men's room, for old time's sake." He winked.

"Wash my hands," I lied. He knew I was lying, too. Butch could always see right through me. I wanted one more look at the sink I'd leaned Mac against, one more flash of a memory I could cherish the rest of my life, however long that was.

# THIRTY-FOUR

THE TWINK WALTZED IN AROUND 9:00 P.M. I knew his type—loud, self-centered, and so light in the loafers just walking with his feet on the ground seemed like a magic trick. We can't say these things today, but back then we weren't so concerned with hurting each other's feelings or what the rest of the world would think if they heard us call someone a fag. It's what they called us. The language police have taken all the fun out of words, but I still like *light in the loafers*, *poof*, and my favorite, *swish*. I knew perfectly well I was one of them, that we were fringe citizens together. Hell, that's the whole history of the mafia and gay bars: we were criminals who needed a place to drink and touch each other, and the mob was pleased to oblige.

"Dick here?" he said, gliding up to the bar. His hair was glaringly platinum and his sequined belt buckle flashed in the bar's low light, riding the top of his hip huggers.

I looked around at the dozen or so customers. "Plenty of it," I said.

"Cute."

"Me or my sense of humor?"

He eyed me quickly up and down. "Both, if I was desperate. But I'm talking about *the* Dick."

"Ah, you're referring to Mr. Montagano. I'm sorry but he hasn't come in yet."

I almost said he only comes in on Wednesdays, but that had changed with the panic surrounding Popper Jack. Business was hurting and Dick had been stopping by at least every other day.

"Drink?" I said.

"I'm surprised you offered after my comment."

The kid was self-aware, that was unusual. "It's my job. Besides, I could use the company." I nodded at the empty barstools.

"Sure, why not? I might as well kill some time. He told me he was going to be here." He took a seat, adjusting himself several times before finding the perfect position. "I'll have a white wine."

I got a glass of wine for him. I didn't bother asking what kind. The Parrot wasn't a bar that stocked pricey wines—you got house red or white, or you went somewhere else.

I walked back to where he was sitting and set the glass down on a napkin.

That's when I saw it. I wasn't sure if I was imagining it or if somehow, in a world of coincidences, this kid with the wispy blond hair and lacerating stare had stumbled into the strangest of them all.

"What are you looking at?" he asked me.

"Where did you get that?"

"Get what?"

"The ring."

There on his right pinky was the jade ring Ben Wennig had worn. I knew it well. I'd sucked on his fingers the night we had sex; I'd had that ring between my lips.

"Oh, this cheap thing," he said, lifting his hand and wiggling his fingers. "Dick gave it to me."

"Dick?"

He scowled at me. "I can see why they call this place the Parrot. Yes, *Dick*. Mr. Montagano. Fat Dick, is what I'm told you call him."

I felt the blood drain from my face and my knees go weak.

"When did he give it to you?" I asked, stepping back from the bar. It was as if I'd been repelled by the ring, the guy who was wearing it, and the implications of where it came from.

"Couple nights ago," he said. "It was my birthday." Leaning forward, he lowered his voice and added, "But I'll tell you what, my blowjobs are worth a lot more than some cheap ring from a pawn shop."

I was expressionless by then. "Is that what he told you? That he bought it in a pawn shop?"

"He called it a jewelry store," he said, rolling his eyes. "But it's dime store trinket crap, he might as well have found it in a dumpster."

A chill ran through me, the sort of sudden, cold current you'd feel if a hand reached out from a grave and grabbed your pant leg.

"I need to go," I said. "Other customers …"

He looked at me like I was emotionally disturbed. "Whatever," he said, lifting his glass and sipping his wine. "I'll wait here for Dick."

"You do that. I think I'll wait for him, too."

He cocked his head at me, curious about what I'd said and what it might mean. Just as quickly he decided it meant nothing, that I meant nothing and my questions about his ring amounted to nothing.

He waved his pinky at me over the rim of his wine glass: ta-ta.

Feeling sick to my stomach, my head overflowing with ideas—each of them sordid and awful—I walked to the other end of the bar and poured myself a shot glass full of bourbon.

"You okay?" Derek asked, looking at me from the cash register.

"No," I replied quietly. "I'm not okay at all."

* * *

"What do you mean, Fat Dick is Popper Jack?" Mac said. "That's crazy, Marshall, even for you."

It was 3:00 a.m. and I was still awake, lying naked in bed with the phone against my ear. Mac was on duty, calling me back from a pay phone somewhere in Hollywood.

"What's that supposed to mean?" I asked, too exhausted to be hurt.

"You broke into a man's apartment. He's found dead in

Griffith Park, and the trunk in his closet is empty. Now you're telling me the guy who may have shot him is a serial killer. This is not rational."

"You think *I'm* Popper Jack? Is that the kind of crazy you're talking about?"

"Not at all, and don't be stupid. Of course you're not Popper Jack. I'm just not convinced Dick Montagano is, either."

I reached for my sixth, or maybe my tenth, cigarette and lit it. Smoking in bed wasn't dangerous when you were wide awake with no chance of falling asleep.

"It was Ben's ring. I recognized it, down to the scratch in the gold on the left side."

He waited a moment, choosing his words. "Has it occurred to you," he said carefully, "that Ben Wennig might have slept around?"

"With Fat Dick?"

"The guy was new in town, you said that yourself. He didn't have a job yet. Maybe he needed some quick cash. You can probably relate to that."

His tone this time was chiding, not affectionate.

"I turned tricks a long time ago," I said, a little too defensively. "It's not my life anymore, Mac, or is it Kevin McElroy, considering the professional distance you need to keep?"

"Listen to me. I know you hustled, it's not a big deal, except that you stayed alive. That matters. I'm just trying to suggest alternatives to how this kid at the bar got a dead man's ring."

"From Fat Dick!"

"Yes, but how did Dick get it?"

"You're hurting my head," I said. "It was all very simple and clear to me when I saw the ring: Fat Dick is Popper Jack. He's a mob lieutenant."

"With a penchant for twinks," he said skeptically.

It stopped me. I didn't know who the earlier victims were, but the three I'd known would not fit that description.

"Maybe he kills against type," I said.

"Listen to yourself, Marshall. Think this through. Remember that Ben Wennig wasn't the first. These killings go back at least three years, maybe more. Whoever he is, he was killing long before some foolish reporter—"

"Now dead."

"—now dead, called him 'Popper Jack.' You're making connections where there aren't any."

"The ring is a connection, Mac."

"Maybe it is, and maybe it isn't."

It was too much for me to process. I fell silent, trying to untangle it all.

"I think this is enough for now," he said. "Can we talk about this more tomorrow?"

"It is tomorrow."

"Marshall, I'm in a phone booth on Vermont Avenue. I need to get back to my job."

"I understand," I said, jealous that his job was more important than comforting me. I was being petulant and ashamed of it.

"No, you don't understand. I can hear it in your voice. But I need to work, and you need to sleep. There's an explanation for this, I promise. Fat Dick is not Popper Jack, it just doesn't compute."

*For a serial killer it does,* I thought, but said nothing.

"I'll call you in the morning. Try to get some sleep in the meantime. If it eases your mind any, I love you."

"And what if it doesn't?"

"I still love you. Now stop smoking and go to bed."

Damn him, he knew me so well, so quickly. Or maybe he'd just heard me exhaling smoke. It didn't matter. I was drained, tired and confused.

"I love you back," I said. "Talk to you tomorrow."

I put the phone in its cradle on the mattress next to me, reached for another cigarette and lit it off the one I'd been smoking. It was going to be that kind of a night.

# THIRTY-FIVE

IT'S RARE FOR ME TO go a night without sleep. Even after my cancer diagnosis, when I worried how many mornings I had left, I didn't *really* lose a night's sleep. Hours here and there, sure, but to not spend one minute unconscious? That's only happened a few times in my life—the night my mother died, the first time I had sex with another man, and the night I realized Fat Dick was a serial killer.

I'd ended my conversation with Mac unsure of myself. Had I worked myself into a paranoid delusion? It was one thing to believe Fat Dick and the Bianchis had killed Phil over his extracurricular activities. It was quite another to think a lieutenant from the last real mafia family left in Los Angeles would do something as brazen, as *crazy*, as kill gay men in some kind of psychotic spree.

*He's been at it for years*, I thought, remembering what Mac had told me. *That's not a spree, that's a career.*

I was relieved to see the sunrise. For me there has never been any time as rife with anxiety as the hour just before dawn. I got up and pissed for what seemed like five minutes, then made coffee and smoked two cigarettes while it brewed. I was always a heavy smoker—I'm not the moderation type, in case it's not evident—and when things got intense it was common for me to light one cigarette off another, sometimes until the ashtray was full.

I had two calls to make. Both were explosive enough to change my life, or possibly end it. Combined, they would create a before and after in my time on this earth. There have been several of those over the years: before my mother died and after she was gone; before I left Indiana, and after I arrived in Hollywood; before AIDS spread its black wings over us, and after I'd found myself out from under its shadow. That was the sort of precipice I stood at when I finished my coffee, lit another cigarette and reached for the phone.

I had Fat Dick's number. Everyone who worked at the Paisley Parrot knew how to reach him, but it was not a number to be dialed casually. You did not call Dick without a very good reason.

And you did not share the number with anyone. If he knew you'd so much as written it down, you could find yourself on the receiving end of a shout or even a fist. Dick and the Bianchis weren't naïve—they knew the Feds were after them. They probably had his private number already, but it was treated like a well-kept secret you divulged at your own risk.

The other call I had to make was to the FBI. I took a deep breath, lit another cigarette, put the phone against my ear and dialed.

* * *

I don't know where Dick was when he answered, because I didn't know where the phone number led to. His home in Encino with his wife and kids? I wondered suddenly how old his children were, and what they were named. *Little Dick*? I thought, and laughed out loud. It was nervous laughter, gallows humor. I doubted the number rang at his home. More likely it was at his Hollywood apartment, the one he said he kept for business but that doubled as a love nest. I laughed again at the idea of Fat Dick Montagano *having* a love nest. Like a big, hairy spider with an alluring smile. I remembered that he was a killer, whether or not he was Popper Jack. He had killed—or ordered the killing of—many men, I was sure of it. And if I was right, he had personally murdered a half dozen gay men.

"Who is this?" the voice said. It was Dick's voice, there was no mistaking it. He was gruff and to the point.

"It's me," I replied, feeling as if my bowels might give out on me.

"Who the fuck is 'me'?"

"It's Marshall, Mr. Montagano."

There was silence as it registered who I was. "Oh, alright. So what do you want, Marshall? To talk about the job?"

He did not say 'the offer' because it hadn't been optional.

"Exactly, yes, that's why I called."

"Good to hear it. But I don't have conversations on the phone, you understand."

He knew there was a real possibility his phone was wiretapped. It went with the territory.

"Of course not," I said. "I just thought I'd call and—"

"Mistake number one," he said. "You don't think. *I* think. And I'll tell you what to think when you meet me at the Parrot this afternoon."

"I'm on shift at six," I said.

"So make it five."

He wanted to talk for an hour? What exactly was he asking me to do besides take over Phil's responsibilities at the bar?

"I have to be somewhere at six," he said, as if he'd read my mind. "I won't take much of your time."

"Oh, okay," I said. "I'll be there, Mr. Montagano."

"You can call me Dick."

It was the way he said it that made my skin crawl. In that instant I imagined him saying that to his victims just before he ended their lives.

"Dick it is, then."

He laughed at that, but I couldn't tell if he was amused or contemptuous. Probably both.

"Be there at five, kid," he said.

I heard the line go dead.

It was time to make my second call.

* * *

I'd left Todd Stanton's business card on the kitchen counter. I could have put it in my wallet, but the card, and what it meant for me, was something I'd wanted kept at a distance.

I stared at it, at the embossed logo. I stared at his name. *Todd Starnes, Special Agent.* I wondered what made an agent special. Maybe he only worked special cases, like mad bombers and mafia chieftains. I held the card in my fingers, reading it repeatedly as if the letters didn't make sense to me. I *wanted* them to not make sense, to fall to the floor and tumble away from me. I wanted nothing to do with the card what it implied for my life, but I had no choice.

Two minutes later I was back on the phone. The number Todd had given me was a direct line—he answered on the second ring.

"Stanton," he said.

"It's a go," I replied, just as abruptly.

"Who is this?"

"Marshall James."

I waited a moment for my name to register with him. That's all it took. Apparently Mr. Todd Stanton, Special Agent, had kept his finger on the 'Go' button and was waiting for the right opportunity, or a call from me. I'd just made his job easier.

"Can you explain what you mean?" he asked.

Although I couldn't hear anything but his voice, I imagined him grabbing a pen and paper, or even waving at his colleague Jim Barnes as he walked past the open door, motioning him into the room to huddle on our next move.

"I have a meeting with Fat Dick this afternoon," I said. "I called him and said I wanted to talk."

"About what?"

"About the job offer. He wants me to take over for Phil Seaton, but he hasn't said what that means."

"Well, well," he said. "Good work, Mr. James."

I almost told him to call me Marshall, then stopped myself.

"So what's next?" I asked. "I set up the appointment. Where do we go from here?"

"What time are you meeting Montagano?"

"Five o'clock. He said it wouldn't take long."

"Can you meet us back at Hollywood Division?"

"Not at the bureau?" I said, unaware of where the FBI had its office in Los Angeles, but certain it had one.

"No, let's meet back at the station. This is a now a joint effort. I'm told the police think Montagano has information about these Popper Jack killings."

*Has information*? I wanted to scream. *He* is *Popper Jack*! I kept the thought to myself, aware at that moment I was at the only person who thought Fat Dick and Popper Jack were the same person.

"Fine," I said instead. "What time should I meet you there?"

He thought about it, then said, "We have to get you wired—"

*Ah, Christ.*

"And give you some very fast, basic training on how to do this—"

*Without getting my head blown off.*

"So let's make it four o'clock. That gives us an hour."

"More like fifty minutes," I said. "I can't be late meeting Fat Dick. Late is a capital offense with this guy."

"Of course. So make it three forty-five. We'll get you on your way by a quarter to five and have plenty of time to put ourselves in position."

*Right,* I thought. That's the other part of this—they'll be sitting in a van outside the Paisley Parrot. Will they hear the gunshot when Fat Dick shoots me? Or my struggle when he strangles me? I always imagined piano wire around the neck to be a quick death followed by decapitation.

"Will Mac be there?" I asked.

"Mac who?"

"Never mind."

"Oh," he said, as it dawned on him who I was talking about. "Detective McElroy, you mean. I honestly don't know. We weren't planning on the LAPD being involved in the surveillance part of this, but if it will make you more comfortable … you know, relax you some …"

Could he have guessed at the relationship between Mac and me? Did his offer demonstrate his tacit *approval* of it? Whatever his reasons for suggesting it, I jumped at the chance to have Mac near me, especially if my life might end in an instant.

Clearing my throat, I said, "I'd like that very much."

Softening his voice, he replied, "We won't tell them why, don't worry about it."

Kindness where you least expect it is a wonderful thing. I started to thank him. He cut me off.

"See you at three forty-five. You can even be a minute late, Mr. James. We're not the mob."

He hung up. I found myself wanting to say more, to speak into the dead air and tell this man how frightened I was, and how much I needed Mac in that van outside, if only to bear witness to the end of my life.

*Don't cry, Marshall. It's not your style.*

After setting the handset back in its cradle, I debated calling Mac. I could give him a heads up, fill him in on the calls with Fat Dick and Todd Stanton. But then he would worry, too. He might want to control things, to insert himself where he wasn't wanted, particularly with the FBI.

I decided it was better to let Special Agent Todd Stanton do the talking and explaining. He would speak to the detectives. He would let Mac know his presence was wanted, most likely in a private conversation. I'd ended my call with Stanton feeling grateful, even if it was based on assumptions about him. Maybe the world wasn't as hard as I'd thought. Maybe there are islands of compassion, and we just spend most of our lives swimming between them.

I glanced at the clock. I had enough time to rest, and maybe even sleep. I laid on the couch, staring at the ceiling, willing oblivion to come for me, if only for an hour. At that point, I'd take what I could get.

## THIRTY-SIX

THE SOUND OF A RINGING telephone assaulted my dream. In it, I'd been having an argument with Mac on a restaurant patio. A large red umbrella flapped above us. The ocean rocked a short distance away to my right, seen over a metal railing. The location made no sense. Were we in Santa Monica? Some other beach town on the coast? The French Riviera? What we were doing there fit only in the logic of dreams. I was telling him I had to go through with this plan ... *for my country? For the men who'd been murdered?* He was gripping my hand with his, insisting I let him take my place, that I let him die for me, when the sound of a phone came crashing through.

I'd set my answering machine to ring seven times in case I was in the bathroom or making dinner in the kitchen. That's the only thing that kept me from sleeping through it. By the fifth ring, I was mostly awake and unhappy about it. The dream, while upsetting, had been part of sleep I'd desperately needed.

I rolled over on the couch and reached for the phone.

"Hello?" I slurred. I sounded to myself the way I did on mornings after a drinking bout, and I felt just as beat up.

"I'm downstairs, kid. Let's go."

It took me a moment to recognize the voice.

"Dick?" I said, hearing the sudden alarm in my voice. "I thought we were meeting at five o'clock."

"Change of plans. Something's come up, I can't meet you at the Parrot, so I came here instead. You dressed?"

It was two in the afternoon, why wouldn't I be dressed?

"Yes, of course."

"What do you mean 'of course'? For all I know you spend your time at home naked."

"Where are you?" I asked, wondering if he was in a

phone booth or if he had one of those new mobile phones I'd seen in a few rich men's cars—satellite phones or something, the size of a bread loaf.

"I told you, kid, I'm downstairs. Don't concern yourself with where. You just come outside and I'll be there. You know my car."

"At the curb?" Highland Avenue by my apartment wasn't a stretch of road where you could easily stop and idle.

"In the building's lot."

"Black Benz," I said, verifying what I already knew.

"I try to keep it understated." He laughed, one of the most unsettling sounds I have ever heard in my life. "And by the way, don't call anybody. I'll know if you did."

Flustered, I said, "I wouldn't call anybody, Dick. Why would you think that?"

He waited a long, terrifying moment, then said softly, "No reason, kid. Just come down. The clock is ticking."

*The clock is ticking*. Words I've always lived by, starting with my mother's death. Life can go along splendidly for a time, sometimes *long periods* of time, then all of a sudden a large rock falls out of the sky and misses your head by an inch. Time ticks, clock hands keep moving, and you learn, as I did when I was young and now when I'm getting old, that the one thing we have of true value—time—gets squandered while we're not even looking. *The clock is ticking*.

I hung up the phone and felt perspiration forming under my arms. Dick had come to my home, which meant he knew where I lived. That was easy enough. I'd filled out tax forms and submitted a flimsy resume when I was hired at the Parrot. But he'd said on the call he couldn't meet me at the bar. *So where are we going*? It was a question with serious implications.

*And by the way, don't call anybody. I'll know if you did.* Was that even possible? Or was it Dick's way of scaring me into complying? How would he knew if I picked up the phone and made a thirty-second call to Mac?

*Take a deep breath, Marshall. Don't imagine things.* I got up and quickly prepared to leave. I kept telling myself this was just a conversation I'd be having with Fat Dick—maybe at a restaurant, or maybe a park where he felt comfortable talking on a bench, away from prying ears and microphones. It was nothing, I told myself. Business had called him away that afternoon, that's why we couldn't meet later. He just wanted to go over the details of my new responsibilities.

I slipped my loafers on, tucked my shirt in, and glanced at the clock. Five minutes had passed since we'd spoken. Would he think I'd defied him and made a frantic call for help? Or that I'd climbed out a window and fled up the street?

I grabbed my keys from my dresser. Next to them sat the pager. I'd been wearing it on my belt when I went out, never wanting to miss a communication from Mac.

For whatever reason, I slipped it into my right sock this time. I instinctively knew it would be a mistake to get into Fat Dick's car with a pager on, but I also knew I'd be a fool to leave it behind.

I got downstairs to the parking lot on the side of the building. There he was, sitting in his black Mercedes, smoking a cigar with the window down. As much as I hated the smell of cigars, I didn't want him to roll the window up. I didn't want to be concealed behind tinted glass, alone in a car with Fat Dick Montagano.

"Get in," he said, without looking at me as I approached from the side.

By then I was less concerned about sweating through my shirt, and more concerned about pissing my pants.

I got in the passenger seat. Some kind of large black phone sat in a holder between us, massive compared to what we call cell phones today. It had a retractable antenna on it.

"Nice," I said, nodding at the phone.

"Shut up, kid. I'll tell you what's nice."

Much to my relief he left his window down. He put the car in reverse and backed out of the spot. I realized we weren't taking Highland Avenue after all. He turned left onto Franklin, and I suddenly had an idea where we were going.

## THIRTY-SEVEN

I KNEW FRANKLIN AVENUE WELL. I'd driven along its winding path many times, climbing up the small hump from Whitley, Grace and Wilcox avenues, down across Cahuenga Boulevard and eastward toward the neighborhood of Los Feliz. I'd had friends living in apartments along this route who were now memories, some more faded than others. I'd also turned a trick or two in buildings I vaguely remembered, with men I'd completely forgotten. On a normal day, riding along Franklin Avenue would be comforting at best, sorrowful at worst, but this was not a normal day. The sun was shining brightly, and I was being driven to an unknown location by Fat Dick Montagano.

The conversation had minimal. He kept puffing his cigar, blowing clouds of tobacco smoke out the driver-side window. I wanted to ask questions but sensed he did not want to talk, at least not in the car.

We crossed Tamarind, then Bronson, and as we approached Canyon Drive, I thought for a moment he was taking me to Phil's apartment. I'd been just two blocks from this corner, crawling into a window in a decision I'd regretted ever since. But we drove past Canyon, past Van Ness, and then, suddenly, we turned left on Taft.

The neighborhood looked as benignly residential as any in the city. There were moderately priced homes with modestly manicured lawns. There was no ostentation in sight, since it wasn't the kind of area that invited it.

As Dick pulled the Benz into a parking spot on the street, I wondered if he owned one of the homes here. I was sure he could afford it, or that the mob could.

"Which one is yours?" I asked, looking out the window at the houses as he turned the ignition off.

"None of 'em," he said. "Let's go, kid."

I was twenty-five and it annoyed me that he kept calling me kid, but it was the least of my concerns. I'd gotten into a car with Fat Dick, something I was sure not everyone before me had survived. Now I was heading somewhere with him and no one knew it. Not the FBI, not Mac, nobody. I was tempted to touch the pager in my sock, just for good luck, but it might draw Dick's attention and put an end to the one trick I had up my sleeve.

We walked along the sidewalk to Franklin Avenue, Dick several steps in front of me—apparently he didn't think I would run down the street screaming for help—then we turned at the corner and walked into the courtyard of a large, brown-brick apartment building. It had a low-rent feel to it, but with a certain budget charm, the kind of address you could afford to live at on a bartender's wages. At the same time, it looked a little like what we call pre-war buildings in New York City, the war being World War II. This one may have been built in the 1950s, I don't know, but its U-shape, with the courtyard and main door flanked by overlooking apartments, had the effect of both protecting us and swallowing us up. Once we walked under the metal arch that connected the sides, there was nowhere to run.

Still saying nothing, Dick took a set of keys from his pants pocket and opened the main door. He held it for me, the closest he came to an act of courtesy.

The lobby was just a large empty room with high ceilings and stone staircases on each side leading up to the apartments. Everything was dark brown, like the building itself. A manager's apartment faced the main door, with a small step leading up to it. To our right was an elevator so old it had a cage across the front you had to pull back to enter. Dick led me to it, opened the elevator and motioned me in.

*Don't go,* my mind screamed. *Do not get in this elevator.*

"What's the matter?" Dick said, still holding the elevator gate opened.

"Nothing, I just ..."

"Let's go, kid. I'm not gonna hurt you, if that's what you're thinking."

"No," I lied. "Not at all." I stepped into the elevator and Dick entered behind me. It was, for the ten seconds it took us to get to the third floor, the most claustrophobic, unpleasant, unforgettable space I have ever been in, and that includes a waiting room with an IV of chemo headed my way.

We got off and turned left—I remember that detail—and walked up the hallway to apartment 3B. Dick fished for another key, slid it into the dead bolt and opened the door to the hideaway I'd only heard about.

"So this is ..." I said, stopping myself as we entered.

"This is what?" he replied, expecting me to finish. He casually reached out and locked the door behind us. It was a sound I've never forgotten.

"I'd just heard you kept a place in the city."

"What else have you heard?" he said.

"Nothing, really."

He led me into the living room.

"Hi, Mr. Bartender with the attitude."

My shock was visible, and audible—I gasped at the sight of the twink sitting in an armchair, his shoeless feet tucked under him as he perched like a bird from hell.

I stopped in my tracks, then felt Dick's palm on my back, prodding me into the living room.

"Hello ..." I stammered.

"Brody," said the twink. "You'd know that if you'd asked my name like a decent bartender would, but I don't think you're decent."

"Shut up," Dick said, causing the twink to curl his lip in a pout.

"Whatever," said Brody, picking at his sock.

"I thought you wanted to talk," I said to Dick, as I allowed myself to be ushered into the room.

"It's okay. Brody won't repeat anything. Isn't that right, Brody?"

The twink pinched his fingers and zippered his mouth in the universal gesture of keeping secrets.

The apartment wasn't impressive. Not much more decoration than a hotel room, except that it had a kitchen and a separate bedroom. There was a couch along one wall, with a window looking out at the Hollywood sign, visible over the roofs of houses and up the hill. No magazines, no books. A large TV with a VCR and a stack of videos was on a cabinet opposite the couch, and the armchair where the twink sat. Everything was beige.

"Have a seat," Dick said. He tossed his keys on a pedestal that was secured in a wall leading to the kitchen. "You want something to drink?"

"Wine for me," Brody said, getting a grunt from Dick in response.

"Instant coffee?" I asked. I wasn't about ask him to make a pot. The sooner we concluded whatever business we were there for, the better.

I heard a cabinet opening in the kitchen, then the rattle of glasses. Moments later, he came back in carrying two glasses with dark liquid in them.

"I was thinking something stronger," he said, holding out one of the glasses to me. "I hear you like bourbon."

"What about my white?" Brody whined.

"Shut up," said Dick. "Go in the bedroom."

"But I wanna watch!" cried the twink.

It was at that point my fear of pissing myself became a certainty. What, exactly, did Satan's nymph want to watch?

"Do what I say," Dick barked.

The twink uncurled his legs, stood up and padded into the bedroom, slamming the door behind him.

"Where were we?" said Dick.

"You'd heard I like bourbon." I wanted to ask him where he'd learned about my drinking preferences. "It's a little early," I said, taking the glass anyway. I did not want to offend this man. "And I have to work."

"Wouldn't be the first time you drank on the job," he

said, and he winked at me.

It was like being winked at by a bear about to eat you.

I tipped the glass back and took a sip. Bourbon, indeed. Good bourbon. I allowed it to warm me, but not to fog my mind. I took a second, small sip, pretending I'd had more than I did, and set the glass on the coffee table.

"You wanted to talk about the job," I said. "Phil's job."

"Is there any other?" he asked, staring at me. "You got anything else going, kid?"

"Of course not." I felt my face flush and hoped it wasn't too obvious. "I'm happy at the Paisley Parrot, it's where I want to be."

Dick took another swallow from his glass, set it next to mine and sat down in the armchair.

"That's good to know. Phil wasn't so loyal."

I did not want to have this conversation. Whatever Fat Dick and the Bianchis wanted from me, I'd hoped it would not involve details. At least not when I wasn't wearing the wire.

"It's terrible what happened to him," I said weakly.

"Hmm," he said. "Any idea why it happened to him?"

"I'm not sure I know what you're getting at, Mr. Montagano."

"No?"

He got up and walked to the cabinet. He leaned down and picked up a remote, then stepped back to give me a view of the TV as he turned it on.

"You like porn?" he asked.

I felt my bowels loosen. This is why he brought me here? To rape me while he watched a sex video?

"I don't own a VCR," I said. "And no, I'm not into porn."

"You ever make any?" he persisted.

I was getting angry. I had no sexual interest in this man, and I was not going to let my guard down in any way.

"I thought we were here to talk about work, whatever it is you want me to do now that Phil's gone."

He turned and looked at me. "And you have no idea what Phil was up to? Is that so, kid?"

"I'm not a kid," I said.

"Fair enough. And you're not into porn. So let's watch something else."

Without changing tapes—which meant he'd had one already loaded into the VCR—he first turned on the TV, then, when the picture was up, he pushed another button on the remote and a tape began to play.

There I was in Phil's bedroom, looking around, making my way toward the closet. The camera had had a tape in it after all, and we were watching it.

"I need to use the bathroom," I said.

"Really? Something upset your stomach, kid?"

There was nothing for Fat Dick to worry about—I could not barricade myself in the bathroom and dial 911 on an iPhone. My options, had I chosen to delay the inevitable, were to brace myself against a door that may not have a lock on it, scream for help, or sit on the floor praying to a God I didn't believe in.

"Go ahead," he said. "Pee, shit, whatever you need to do. But don't take too long. And by the way, there's no window in there, this isn't Phil's place."

I nodded, got up and hurried into the bathroom. Once inside, I closed the door behind me. It did not have a lock, which would have been nearly useless anyway. I reached down and yanked the pager out of my sock.

Trying to remain as calm as possible, I thought quickly of what I could page. HELPME might mean nothing to Mac, and only upset him. It would be a plea for help without any location, any way to find me. I punched in 3283425. I didn't know if he would decipher it, or if he could in time to do anything about it. FATDICK. And then a second page, 27832, APT3B. Finally a third page: 435763. HELPME. It was all I could do.

"You okay in there?" Dick said through the door. "I don't hear anything."

I stuffed the pager back into my sock and flushed the toilet. I opened the door, and there he stood, smiling at me.

"Let's have that conversation," he said.

It was my chance to stall. If I could get him talking about the Parrot, about whatever they wanted from me, I could buy precious minutes. They had the videotape of me searching Phil's bedroom. They had, I was now certain, the cash and the drugs. And they had put an end to Phil. It was only business, something to negotiate.

I remembered the twink in the bedroom. What had he wanted to watch? Me having sex with Fat Dick? That would explain why I'd been brought here. It could also buy me precious time.

We walked back into the living room. I sat on the couch while Dick remained standing.

"Finish your drink," he said.

It was an order. I took my glass from the coffee table and guzzled the bourbon. At that point there was no reason not to. I needed the liquid courage in a way I'd never needed it before.

After swallowing the last of it, I gave Fat Dick my best come-hither look and said, "I've always had a thing for you, Dick."

He smiled. "A thing for me, Dick, or a thing for *my* dick?" He laughed at his own joke.

He finished his bourbon, then said, "Let's get a refill." He took our glasses and walked back into the kitchen.

Perhaps that was the moment I needed, the one in which I could run to the door, throw the deadbolt and make it out of the apartment. But was it the right move? And could I really escape? Dick had a gun somewhere, I was sure of that, possibly on his person. Would I be shot in the back as I ran down the stairs? Or had he brought me here to talk about the job, and once we had, he would drop me off at the Parrot or just tell me to walk there?

I heard the bedroom door open, as if on cue. Brody came shuffling back into the room and took the same seat he'd had before, curling his feet up under his legs and smiling at me.

"So you liked my boy's ring."

I jumped. Somehow Dick had come back into the living room while I was staring at the twink, who lifted his hand and wiggled Ben Wennig's jade ring at me.

*Oh my God,* I thought. *The twink – Brody – knows all about it. He's known about it all along.*

Dick was standing behind me. He reached over me and offered me the glass. It was nearly full this time, enough bourbon that, had I consumed it, I would not be able to stand. It didn't matter. I now knew this was the last location I would ever be seen alive in.

"It's a pretty color," I said. I could hear the flatness in my own voice, sense the distance I was even then creating between myself and reality.

"You recognized it, right?" said Brody, waving the ring at me again.

"Oh yes."

I turned to face Dick. I wanted to look into his eyes.

"But what I don't understand is why."

"You mean *why you,*" he said.

I nodded.

"I've had my eye on you for a while, kid. I used to see you on the boulevard – "

"Santa Monica."

"What other fucking boulevard is there? Of course, Santa Monica."

"I was new in town. I'm not a hustler."

He snorted. "Hustle, don't hustle, I don't care. My boy doesn't hustle anymore, do you?

"Never, Poppy!" Brody said. "Not since I met you."

"He does help me, though," Dick added, not saying what it was Brody helped him with. I was beginning to imagine.

"Then you started working at the Parrot. Not just drinking there, *working* there. And I could not believe my luck. I couldn't take my eyes off you."

"Why didn't you ... approach me sooner?" I asked, knowing now he'd killed at least six other men at his whim, and he'd had help with at least some of them.

"I don't know," he said. "That's the funny thing about what I do. It has to be perfect, you know? I have to know the moment is exactly the right one."

"Like it is now," Brody said. "Right, Poppy?"

"Right you are, Button."

*He calls his accomplice in serial murder 'Button'?* Unable to stop myself, I laughed out loud.

"What the fuck is funny to you?" Dick said, his hand swinging out and slapping me on the head.

"Hit me again and I'll ..."

"What, kid? What are you going to do?"

"Yeah, asshole," said the twink. "What are you going to do?"

I will never know what possessed me, what source of strength made itself available to me at that precise moment, but something did.

"I know you're Popper Jack," I said. "A sick fuck who kills men for pleasure. And now I know you have a twisted little freak for a sidekick. The cops know it, too, about you anyway.

"Oh, and the FBI. They know all about me breaking into Phil's apartment and what I found there. They know about the camera with the missing videotape. As a matter of fact, *Fat Dick*, I'm wearing a wire."

He hurled his glass across the room, smashing it against the wall as bourbon splattered on everything in sight.

I knew I was going to die, and I didn't care. I would not die whimpering.

In motions faster than I knew humanly possible, Dick yanked his belt out of his pants and lunged at me. I want to say I pivoted away from his grasp, that I was faster and better, but that would be a lie. The next thing I knew he was on top of me, both of us on the floor. The coffee table had been knocked over as we fell onto the carpet.

The twink leapt out of his chair, knelt down and stared at me, inches from my face. Is this what Ben had seen just before he died? And Freddy, and Brad Herring?

Dick was on top of me, straddling my chest. His face was scarlet, spittle flying from the corners of his mouth.

He took the belt, one end tightened in each fist, and wrapped it around my neck so fast I didn't know what was happening.

My life did not flash before my eyes. That's just wishful thinking by people with the time to die properly, or not die at all. I did not have that luxury. A large, furious, homicidal killer was on top of me and there was nothing I could do but claw at the belt tightening around my neck.

"I'll let you pass out a few times," he said. "That's the best, kid."

"The best!" sang Brody, followed by a peal of laughter.

"You just about go unconscious, then I bring you back for some more. I'll get what I want. Maybe before you're dead, maybe after."

"After! *Please*!" shrieked Brody.

"Then I'll show up at the Parrot waiting for you. We have a meeting scheduled. But guess what? You never get there."

I'd managed to hook my fingers under the belt. I tried my hardest, my mightiest, to loosen it, knowing it was impossible.

I closed my eyes, refusing to let the face of Richard Montagano and his platinum blond gargoyle be the last thing I saw. I thought of Mac. His smile. His amazing eyes. His body. His smell. His touch. I felt tears begin to stream down my face.

Then I heard thunder as the door to the apartment blew inward.

## THIRTY-EIGHT

"FREEZE, MOTHERFUCKER!" THE COMMAND WAS loud and irresistible. There was no room in it for possibilities other than surrender. And it was Mac's voice shouting it.

One instant I was on the outer edge of consciousness, about to slip into oblivion with a belt clenched tightly around my neck; the next instant I was gasping for breath, the belt fallen from Fat Dick's hands.

Through blurry eyes I looked up and saw Dick rise backward, still straddling my chest. His hands flew above his head, instinctively taking the position of a man staring at the barrel of a cop's gun.

The twink instantly tried to play the part of a victim, throwing himself backward as if he'd been struck.

"I tried to help him ..." he squealed. He jabbed an accusing finger at Dick, "This man tried to kill us both!"

Mac ignored him, his attention focused on Dick. "Get off him!" he yelled. I heard footsteps pouring into the room. He wasn't alone.

The next thing I knew, Fat Dick was sitting on the floor beside me, his hands clasped behind his head. The twink had backed himself up against a wall and was whimpering, trying his best to be a desperate puppy.

"He broke into my apartment," Dick said, nodding at me, careful to keep his hands where the cops could see them. "I came home and caught him. Piece of shit was stealing my TV. I got him on tape breaking into that dead guy's apartment, too. He probably killed him."

It didn't occur to Dick that the police would want to know why and how he had video from Phil's bedroom.

I managed to roll over, squint, and clear my vision enough to see that Mac had arrived with backup: detectives Dean Randall and Rita Crescent had come in just behind him, guns raised.

"Shut the fuck up," Mac said, hurrying behind Dick and handcuffing him. "He wasn't stealing anything but your freedom, asshole. You're going to prison for this one."

"And his bitch," I said, pointing at Brody. "They're in it together."

"Liar!" shrieked Brody.

Mac ignored him. "Cuff blondie over there," he said to Rita.

"Going to prison for what?" demanded Dick. "For defending myself?"

"He has the videotape," I said, confirming what Dick had claimed moments earlier. I'd managed to speak despite a windpipe that felt crushed. For all I knew it had been and I'd be recuperating for months, never able to speak above a whisper again.

"Tape of the killings?" It was Rita, her gun held steady on Brody while Dean cuffed his hands behind his back. Mac yanked Dick up off the floor.

"No," I said. "Or maybe, I don't know what's on all those tapes. But the one in the VCR is from Phil Seaton's apartment." I didn't care if I incriminated myself in a burglary. I hadn't stolen anything, and I needed to be certain they connected Dick to Phil's murder.

"Don't touch those tapes," Dick howled. "Don't touch anything in here. I've got my rights. I want a lawyer!"

"You'll get your lawyer," Mac said, "and we'll get a warrant, you can count on that. We'll get whatever we need, Dick. Or is it Popper Jack?"

I could see the shock on Fat Dick's expression. The realization that they were after him for the murders of Ben, Freddy, Brad and more, hit him in that moment like punch in the face.

"I don't know what the fuck you're talking about," Dick said, when clearly he knew what Mac was talking about and it scared the crap out of him.

"Take him away," Mac said.

Rita holstered her service pistol, stepped forward and grabbed hold of Dick's arm. He was big enough to cause trouble, but with his wrists held in handcuffs and his mind in a state of worried frenzy, he wasn't going to put up a fight. Dean pulled Brody off the floor with such force it could have broken his arm.

They both waited a moment to see what Mac wanted them to do. It had never been clear to me who gave the orders.

"Load them in the car," Mac said. "And call a bus for Marshall."

By 'bus' I knew he meant ambulance. "I'm fine," I said. "I just need water."

"You're not fine."

Dean followed Rita out of the apartment as they dragged Fat Dick and Brody with them.

We were alone now. I'd become fully aware of my surroundings, hyper-aware, and I realized I'd pissed myself. It's the kind of thing that happens when you're being strangled.

Mac could see shame on my face as my hand slid down to my pants, feeling the wetness.

"Don't worry about it," he said. "You're alive. That's all that matters. That and the fact I love you."

He glanced around briefly to be sure the others had left. Then he stepped up to me, pressed himself against me, and kissed me as hard as I have ever been kissed before or since.

"I don't know what to say," I managed, feeling tears begin again.

"Say you love me, Marshall James."

"I love you, Mac McElroy."

He stepped back, clearing his throat. I could see wetness in his eyes. The mighty Mac, Protector Mac, *my* Mac, was on the verge of tears. But I knew it was a line he wouldn't cross that night, if he ever did.

"Sit on the couch and wait," he said. "The paramedics will be here any minute."

I looked at the couch and frowned. It was the last place I wanted to put my body, back on a couch where I'd been attacked. Mac could tell from my reaction what I was thinking.

"The floor, then," he said. "Just sit, please."

I heard footsteps and voices. The paramedics had arrived and were rushing up the stairs.

Lowering his voice, Mac looked at me and said, "And don't you ever come that close to leaving me again."

I let myself go then, falling into a heap on the floor. The tears came back, this time flowing freely. I had almost died. I had almost left Mac. I had almost been another victim at the hands of a sadist. Almost … but not quite.

I felt an oxygen mask being slipped over my face, hands checking my pulse, and, thankfully, a needle of something soothing being slipped into my arm.

I let them take me. I wanted to rest.

It was over.

## THIRTY-NINE

FAT DICK WASN'T LUCKY ENOUGH to die resisting arrest. By the time of his trial six months later, I'm sure he would have preferred death by cop to the spectacle of being held to account in front of the world. The media had its feeding frenzy, descending from far and wide onto the Los Angeles courthouse. There were reporters from Paris and Berlin, as well as from Chicago and Phoenix. If you spent five minutes in the journalists' area, you'd hear almost as many languages as were spoken in the entire city at the time. The arrest and trial of Popper Jack, as he was known by then across the civilized world, was bigger news than the Olympics headed our way in a year.

Not only was Richard Montagano now the most famous mob figure L.A. had ever seen, eclipsing the bosses he worked for and those who had come before, but he was also the serial killer du jour: Popper Jack, heinous, monstrous stalker of gay men who had claimed the lives of the innocent for at least six years. And while it stung knowing not everyone considered his victims innocent, the majority of citizens believed Fat Dick, Richard Montagano, Popper Jack, *whatever you called him,* was a devil straight from Hell who should be sent back there. It didn't matter that he would never see the inside of an execution chamber in California; making sure he got sent on his way was satisfaction enough—and the only outcome most of us wanted.

Meanwhile, the twink, Brody Gallagher, took a plea deal in exchange for testifying against Fat Dick. He'd only been in on the murders starting with Ben, and he swore he'd simply acted as a lure. I didn't believe a word he said, least of all that Ben, Freddy and Brad all got taken by someone as evil and cruel as Brody. I preferred thinking they'd been caught unaware, snatched off the sidewalk or called over to a car door for assistance, with Dick waiting inside to grab them. It didn't matter, really. Brody had helped in whatever way he could, enjoying every second of it, and three men I knew were dead. The only one they hadn't killed was me.

Eileen Montagano—Dick's wife—took her kids and moved away. She did not stand by her man, she did not stick around to see what happened. Her first reaction, caught on camera by the media hounds, was to be more shocked that he was gay than that he *killed* gay men. Goodbye and good riddance, Eileen.

As is often the case in serial homicides, the accused was brought to trial facing just one count of murder. Sometimes it's more—maybe two or three victims out of, say, twenty—but in Dick's case he was charged with the murder of Ben Wennig. Poor Ben. Innocent Ben. Ben who had arrived in Hollywood more wide-eyed and vulnerable than I had, and whose ring sealed Dick's fate. Dick had been arrogant enough to think he could take the ring from a dead man's hand—a man he had strangled and left in a dumpster—and give it to his treacherous boy toy without any concern about its origins. Or maybe that had been their plan all along: to wave the ring at me in the bar and hook me, just like they'd hooked the others. I never knew, and Dick never said. By the time Brody walked into the Parrot, they both thought they could get away with anything.

I was spared having to testify. Brody did that part for me. And while Dick was only charged with one murder, the jury was treated to lurid details of the others that fed an international audience's appetite for shocking description. The prosecutors managed to get it all in, despite wrangling from the defense attorneys and a perturbed but sympathetic judge.

Two months after the trial began, it ended. Richard Montagano was convicted of killing Ben Wennig. He was then sentenced to death, a sentence that was all but symbolic in the Golden State. Appeals, and an odd determination by California to drag its executions out to the point of irrelevance, assured that Dick would die in a death row cell or the infirmary, but not with a needle in his arm.

No one celebrated.

## REMISSION

MEMORY IS AN UNTRUSTWORTHY COMPANION. The things we swear happened—how they happened, in what order, who said what—must be viewed with gentle skepticism. I can say, but not swear, that everyone was satisfied with Fat Dick's conviction. I could say we moved on, and that would be true, but I cannot testify to the sequence of events. Who died before whom, what argument pushed Mac and me to the boiling point. Did we commit our lives to each other and then move in together, or were we living together when we promised to love and to cherish forever and ever?

The good news is that Butch survived. He was one of the lucky ones. I've come to believe that all who live another day are the lucky ones, but that life itself is a luckless affair. I could have died at twenty-five on the floor of a serial killer's apartment, or ten years later when I'd lost another twenty friends and the term 'long term AIDS survivor' was just gaining traction, or three years ago when Dr. Lydia Carmello assured me I had six months to live. Having outlasted so many people, am I a lucky one?

Looking out my window at dusk, breathing in the air from Ninth Avenue, I'm struck again by life's refusal to be neatly ordered. *I was just a kid, really*. Twenty-five? What is it like to be twenty-five? I don't remember. I just remember things that happened.

By the time Richard Montagano was sentenced to death, a sentence we all knew would never be carried out, I'd left the Paisley Parrot. And so had the Bianchis. Their time in the shadows was up. Decades of a weakening mob presence in the City of Angels had come to an ignominious end, replaced by gangs, crack cocaine and criminal enterprises less concerned with codes and mob family loyalty than they were with brutal, efficient success. There were plenty of other bars to work in, bars without ghosts hovering in the corner, waiting to follow me home after last call. I couldn't stay there, and I didn't.

The other big thing that happened by the end of the trial was that Mac and I were an item, a couple, and everyone knew it. I'll give him that: Kevin McElroy was a pioneer. An openly, proudly, gay member of the Los Angeles Police Department. It wasn't easy. Not all of his colleagues—maybe not most of them—were ready to have someone on the Force who didn't consider his love life to be 'nobody's business.' Only gay people are expected to treat our relationships as personal matters that shouldn't be shared publicly. Mac was having none of it. He had my picture on his desk. He talked to me on the phone without lowering his voice. He said, "I love you," quickly and often.

I'm going to stop there. Talking about Mac remains a subject that still touches the pain in my soul. The loss of my mother, the loss of my friends, my own close brushes with death—all these things can weigh on me, but only Mac and the memories of him can rip me open. So let's move on.

Boo is on his way over. We'll watch TV and have dinner from the Chinese place on 38th Street. And we'll have a talk because he wants to. I've felt a change coming for some time now. When you've been with someone for ten years, you can read them as quickly as you can see something different in a room you inhabit every day. It's not a bad thing, I'm sure of it. What I suspect is that, like Mac McElroy all those years ago, he's coming to tell me we need to blend our lives, to sleep and wake together every day. I was supposed to be dead two years ago, and that's just from the cancer. If you factor in all the dangerous situations I've been in, plus AIDS waiting around every corner, plus the murders—and there are more to tell you about—you might think I'm already dead and you're listening to a ghost.

But I'm not a ghost. I'm alive, and strangely thrilled to be. I'm looking forward to Boo giving me an ultimatum he's been holding back for months. And I'm just as certain I'll say yes.

The time is always now, and the time has come.

## A NOTE FROM MARK

Thank you for taking a ride on the imagination train, I hope you've enjoyed the scenery and the company. If you have a moment to write a review that would be much appreciated. Even a few sentences help other readers discover the books and meet the characters.

You can find me at my website, MarkMcNease.com, and also on Twitter (@MyMadeMark), Facebook and Goodreads. I'm always happy to hear directly from readers as well, and I answer every email, so don't be shy, drop me a note any time at Mark@MarkMcNease.com.

If you'd like to be kept up on the next book, please join my email list. Emails are kept strictly confidential and only used for book and author news.

Writing is both my passion and my pleasure, and by the time you read this I'll be working on the next story ... and the next.

Yours from the thickening plot,

Mark.

Made in the USA
Thornton, CO
02/13/24 10:23:14

4e3ff260-1315-4395-8e66-f83abca27ff1R01